PRAISE FOR JERRY RESURRECTED

"This is a perfect book to enjoy for a warm and fuzzy, poignant tale of second chances. The author draws you in until you know there truly is a reason why things happen the way they do." – *Lynn Boire*

"An inspiring and uplifting take on the romance novel. Suki Lang brings together an unlikely pair who at first seem to share little more than a mutual adoration of a small canine companion. Through compelling dialogue, the author reveals the kindness, cruelty and aspirations of her characters along with the losses and disappointments that confine them. She unravels the stirring journey of two families moving from dysfunction to the promise of a shared future." – *Gail Davidson*

"I very much enjoyed reading Jerry Resurrected. You describe quite believably, how easy it is for someone to become homeless as a result of grief, depression, loss of job. I love the most important role Jack the dog plays throughout the novel. It is Jack who everybody loves, bringing them all together. You describe this little wiry dog so well Suki." – *Marsha Bergen*

Jerry Resurrected

A novel by Suki Lang

…where everything happens for a reason

dedicated to –

my granddaughters, Mary Margaret & Jessica Jane

...to you Roy, for all your bright ideas; keep them coming.

To Jason of course ... and to Geoff, to Dave and to Pearl

CHAPTER ONE

Pelting rain snakes its way into the back of Jerry's up-turned collar as he leans into the outdoor rubbish bin. Pulling the jacket tight and grasping it with one hand at his throat, Jerry reaches the other hand as deep down into the bin as he can stretch. He feels the neck of another bottle just out of reach. So far today has been a good one for bottles and cans.

All his clothes are saturated right through, making him cold from head to foot. As soaked as he is, even while draped over the edge of a garbage can, he feels the pride of productivity deep inside.

His pride is what keeps him going on days like this one; a bit of competition with his own self never hurt either. Three trips to the depot so far today and at least one more trip to go if his luck keeps up.

Jerry tells the small white dog at his side, "By my esti-mate we'll have at least one hundred bucks at the end of the day." Between the pop can stash the little kid pointed out, and that roll of copper he found lying right out in the open of an alleyway in the early hours, it has been a good haul.

In the next trash can he comes to, his hand feels the touch of a knotted plastic bag. Giving it a quick lift, he feels the soft pull of fabric inside. But before he can get it open, a small rip is enlarged by the weight of heavier contents within and it splits wide open. Out spills a colourful mass into the mud of the lane.

"Rats," says Jerry to his dog as he bends to pick through the loot, "not much good to us if it's all a bloody muddy mess is it Jack?" The little dog does not make a sound but keeps his eyes firmly on his human friend while Jerry speaks.

Stubby white tail jittering Jack cocks his head to the left, then to the right. Jerry laughs while the dog continues to rock his body from side to side shifting his weight from foot to foot. He gives Jerry a grin of pointy white teeth then shakes the water from his back - head to toe.

The wetness looks like bits of shattered glass as it shoots off the little body in all directions. He shakes so hard all four feet lift off the ground. The wee dog appears to levitate for just a moment.

Noticing as if for the first time, the rain coming down full force, Jerry casts a long assessing look up into the sky. Scanning dark clouds for one spot of sunlight coming their way, he sees none.

It is time to get Jack indoors to towel them both dry. Gathering his bottles, Jerry heads off to collect his final payment for a long mornings work. On his way back out of the depot doorway, which ought to be one stop before home, Jerry sees the little lady for the first time.

She stands outside a bus shelter in the heavy rain; dressed in a style rarely seen these days thinks Jerry to himself. On her perfectly curled dark head, she wears an old-fashioned transparent plastic rain bonnet. The type of rain shield that folds into a fan, then can be neatly squared up to put in the side pocket of a raincoat.

He has not seen the likes of one since the early years of his marriage. His wife had one handy when she caught the bus to school all those years ago. The shelter is crammed full of young people seeking a dry spot to stare at their hand-held digital screens.

In the good old days, a woman would not be left standing in the rain. She would be ushered under cover and given a seat if there was one. Next to her stands a wheeled shopping cart with a tartan cover. And it is the cart that catches Jerry's eye.

He could use something like that for his bottles; or something even bigger. Lugging them around slung over his back is getting tiring. Without warning his little dog Jack, suddenly spots the lady too.

Off he dashes to say hello as if to an old friend. Jumping up, his dirty feet mark her tan raincoat. The lady calmly removes a navy wool scarf from her neck, bends at the waist, smiling, she gives his wet fur a little rub.

So tender is the moment between dog and woman Jerry almost forgets to shout, "Jack! Off!" Heads turn his way. The man in soaked and soiled canvas bomber jacket is barreling toward the dog and the woman. He makes an unsuccessful grab to tug the dog off the lady.

Repeating in a firmer voice he shouts, "Jack! Off! Jack off, Jack off. Jack... Listen now – Jack - off." Sniggers of laughter heard from the comfort of the shelter; from some soul not glued to their screen. Angry grumbling about the homeless bum and his worthless dog is heard too.

Jack jumps clear of Jerry's outstretched hand almost

going into the road. Jerry makes an awkward grab for the dog, bumping the lady in his attempt. A voice from inside the shelter booms, "Hey! Careful man!"

The lady bends over at her waist again, this time coaxing the white fur ball close. She scoops him up in her arms with not a thought of mud or wet on her coat. She allows her face to be licked before handing him back to Jerry and commenting, "What a nice little dog, is he yours?"

"Yeah, yeah he's mine; sorry he jumped on you." Was all Jerry said. He did not like to be a spectacle and wanted to just fade away. But before he could make his escape the lady leaned in for a whisper and pressed a bill into Jerry's jacket pocket, "Here, buy your dog a treat. On me."

The bus pulls up just then giving Jerry no chance to say, he is not a pan handler or hustler of some sort. It is the first time, in a long time, that Jerry cares what another human thinks of him at all.

He wants to ask; who does she think owns the little dog if not him? And he wants to tell this dear lady he is not what she sees at all. Jerry is so much more. On his way back toward what he calls his laneway pad the day's money heavy in his hand, Jerry makes one more stop and takes Jack into a pet store.

"HELLO, YOU TWO!" shouts a voice from behind the counter. "I can see you've had a wet one today. Is it time you bought little Jackie a raincoat?"

I can just see him Jerry silently scoffs but keeps his thoughts on the matter to himself. This will be the first full winter with Jack by his side. Unsure how much of a constant outdoors man Jack will prove to be he asks, "Well I wonder what a coat would cost me?"

Shaking her head Gert tells him, "Oh no Jerry, don't get one here. They are too expensive, and you can find just what Jack needs at the second hand. Want me to give them a call for you?"

Without answering, Jerry casts his eye around looking for the coat section. Spotting it, he makes his way toward the back of the tightly packed store. Over his shoulder he says, "Jack deserves a new one. Don't you Jackie boy?"

Gert still is not so sure because of the cost but goes along just to give advice on size and durability. "Not that one you've got there, Jerry. Jack needs something rain proof. Oh, and a bit of lining would go a long way to keep him warm when the weather gets colder."

With a side long glance, she asks, "By the way, have you found somewhere more permanent to stay Jerry?" Irritated by the question and having had enough of Gert's education on dog coats, Jerry makes a hasty retreat from the jacket rack. Pawing through the dog treat section instead; he grabs the usual and is about to pay when he notices the leashes.

He does not like how Jack had just run off back there. "You know what Gert; Jack just had a narrow escape on Broadway. A leash is what I will get today. I like that bright blue one - but is it going to be long enough? I need something with a bit of length. Or two leashes, I can tie them together."

Casting her eyes around the shop Gert takes on a mystified trance like look … Her breadth has grown so much over the years movement in the small shop has to be calculated for even a very slim customer, to maneuver.

Spotting what she is looking for she reaches up and brings down a leash saying, "You can have this one Jerry. It's been in the store for ages. It is got to be twelve feet or fifteen, I am not sure. Will that do?"

Holding up her hand to fend off objections she says, "Don't worry Jerry you can work it off - it's not a giveaway! I am going to throw in that blue sweater you were holding onto as well and a raincoat. The sweater will keep Jack warm indoors on an evening.

"If you'd just break down all the cardboard in the back storeroom and get it out to the recycle bin in the alley that would be great. Young Melissa is AWOL again. And I can barely squeeze through the doorway to use the facilities, the room is so tight back there."

Melissa had been hired a while back and often could not be counted on to turn up for her shift. Gert is known for helping the demoralized even back when Jerry had his own life together. She has her hand bitten often but as she says, "It's my way of doing something good for someone else."

Gert inherited the building the pet store is housed in, about forty years before. There are two street level businesses with apartments above. Gert lives in one of the apartments. She has never been married but has a daughter who is all grown up now.

Her daughter, a lawyer, practices criminal law; that is how Gert meets many of the Melissa's of the world. Like mother, daughter Claire is just as much a humanitarian and even more of a do-gooder. Always insisting her mother hire from a pool of her jobless clients.

Pointing at a basket behind the counter Jerry says one word to Jack, "Sleep." Immediately obeying, Jack goes around to lay as still and calm as can be in the well-used dog bed that lays ready and kept warm by the aid of a small heater Gert keeps pointed at her feet on a chilly day like this. Taking off his jacket, Jerry hooks it to hang above the heater on a nail in the wall. He holds a dim hope it will dry off a bit while he goes to work in the backroom.

Utter chaos greets him as he sidles past several unpacked boxes. His speed and sense of organization aid him in getting the cardboard crushed and out the door. There is so much stuff lying around the backroom he feels sick that once again Gert is paying for a job poorly done. This is not the first time he has organized her backroom; he knows it will not be the last.

Every time she gets a new helper the first thing they do, is to toss the joint looking for goods to sell. Calling out he asks, "Gert - when was the last time you were in here to have a good look?"

"Oh, I don't know, could be six months... Why do you ask?" Exiting the room Jerry stands in front of Gert, arms folded across his chest ready for a fight. "If you have not seen what's back there lately, I'm going to drive my van up to the door in the lane and turf most of it at the dump. No arguments!"

Laughing Gert just shakes her head, "I'm sure all the good stuff is gone; go for it. And thank you Jerry. Let me know how much the dump fee is and I will reimburse you.

"Wait - hang on a second and I'll phone them. I'm fairly sure if you get there between certain hours, you'll get a better price." Jerry waits while Gert tries to get a live person on the line. Hands in pockets he watches Jack while he waits. And Jack watches Jerry right back.

Jerry read in the paper once the relationship between dog and owner is a symbiotic one; the headline read, Scientists have found that dogs and owners both experience surges in oxytocin; the love hormone. He had no doubt it was true; he feels love vibrating between them right now. Jack came along into his life at just the right moment.

Jerry's thoughts of love are interrupted when Gert hangs up the phone and says, "Just as I thought - between nine in the morning and noon is a set rate for that junk. If you do not mind, I would like you to go to the one in Langley. I have a pickup I'd like you to do out that way too. I will pay you today for the dump fee, forty bucks for your gas and reimburse you when you get back, for the time it takes. I want it done tomorrow though; is that ok?"

Before Jerry can answer Gert sticks her hand out holding a set of keys for him to take. "Here you go - the spare set of keys. Let yourself in tomorrow morning and get an early start. Oh - do you remember how to use the alarm - Just punch in your birth year. It's still in the system since you last used it."

Jerry wonders how many spare keys Gert has handed over. And how many codes she has in her system. It amazes him she has never been out right robbed before. Gert seems very naïve to Jerry.

As if she can read his mind, she tells him he is the only one she completely trusts with the keys and a special code. "Well of course Claire has a key and a code too, but you know what I mean Jerry."

Before heading out the door Jerry hooks the new leash on Jacks collar. The collar looks dingy next to the new leash and Jack looks like a prisoner with his tail at half-mast. The little dogs head is sunk so low it almost touches the floor.

But when Jerry opens the packet of treats, Jack's head and tail both shoot up in full alert. "Here you go, catch." says Jerry. Before putting his jacket back on Jerry attaches the leash to the belt holding up his pants. Once outside the door, instead of walking at Jerry's side like he usually does, Jack zooms ahead tugging on the leash.

Jerry stands still. Jack relaxes. Jerry walks on. Jack pulls again, Jerry stops, Jack relaxes and so it goes for a couple of hundred feet down the sidewalk until Jack gets the message and stops pulling. Finally slowing down to Jerry's pace, they walk as one, side by side. Jerry holds onto the slack of the leash so his little dogs' legs, do not get tangled up.

CHAPTER TWO

Before going into his laneway pad Jerry makes a stop on the back porch of his landlady, Mrs. Bergen. It is a weekly routine to get her garbage and compost bins out to the lane, ready for pick up the next day. Climbing the back-stairs, he fishes the rent envelope out of his pocket and slips it through a letter slot Mrs. Bergen has in her back door.

A back-door mailbox may be a bit unconventional. But there was a time before her husband died, rooms in the basement were rented to other out of luck souls. And the slot was handy to stuff envelopes of rental cash through. Ever since Jerry lost his condo parking spot, he rents her garage out back.

He gets a good rent of $100 a month. Plus, he takes out her garbage and mows her lawn, front and back. Shovelled the walkway when it snowed and once this year, he cleaned all the windows, and the gutters too.

Mrs. Bergen rarely speaks to Jerry but has an odd and very welcome habit of placing a basket out for him once a week. Usually it holds his mail, a small, covered bucket of her homemade soup and the local free newspaper. Like clockwork the basket and all its contents are set out on a table by the back door on the afternoon before garbage day.

Today the added surprise of homemade biscuits is waiting next to the soup. Gathering up his goodies Jerry heads down the stairs to unlock his own door. The garage has two entries. One big electric door from the lane and the other is a side door, just next to the backyard gate.

Jerry keeps the lawn mower and yard care gear under the protection of a lean-to. The garage itself is for his personal use. He feels lucky each time he clicks on the overhead lights.

Backed in and as close to the far wall as possible sits his home on wheels. A 1965 Volkswagen Van, complete with peace sign and flowers his wife hand painted before they travelled across Canada back in the day. Straight out of high school the van was a grad gift from Jan's Mum and Dad.

Jan's parents had no idea she would head off with Jerry for the summer, but she did. What a trip they had. That was the first time they talked about having kids. It was decided to have just one because more than one would not fit in the van.

By the time they returned, with Jan's parents as furious as can be, Jan was pregnant with the boy who would be the centre of Jan's universe. And just as they planned on that cross Canada trip Jordan was an only child.

Every time Jerry enters the garage and catches sight of the painted van, he is thrown back to that summer. And all the years that followed. In so many ways Jerry knows how lucky he had been at one time.

A beautiful smart wife, a son he adored. But now all that is gone, except the van. Bending down he picks up his little dog to begin the chore of drying him off and wiping him clean before he is allowed inside the VW.

Adjacent to the van, against the opposite wall is a long folding table. This is where Jerry sorts his finds of the day, where he prepares his meals. Today he uses it as a surface Jack can stand on while his hair gets dried.

The Bergen garage is the best on a back lane dotted with falling down garages from the nineteen-twenties and thirties. "In original shape too," many would boast with a laugh of pride. When Mr. Bergen was alive, he used it in all seasons. A place to do his woodworking where he was protected from the elements.

He tripped the place out with insulation and electric wall hung heaters and in one corner behind a curtain was a toilet sitting next to an old laundry sink with running water: both hot and cold.

This suited Jerry's need to keep his body clean and his dog's feet rinsed off before getting in the van. And Mrs. Bergen did not seem to bat an eye at the cost of electricity; just paying the bills as they rolled in.

Last winter it was so cold some days he wondered how many dollars her bill would increase during his struggle to fend off pneumonia. Mr. Bergen had ingeniously fashioned long snakes of sand filled, moisture proof fabric, to lie along the garage floor in front of both the side door and the garage door. They did a good job of keeping heat in and a stream of freezing air out. Jerry feels a lot luckier than most people who wind up in this condition of no conventional home to call one's own.

Jerry has another year before he will get his Canada Old Age Security, his other pensions and a Registered Retirement Savings Plan. When that money starts rolling in, he will be well off. Living like this does not worry him at all. He has everything he needs; a daily purpose, a roof over his head, food, and someone to love.

Without the latter he would be sunk for sure. It is his dog Jack who really makes living in this new reality tolerable. Without Jack the joy he feels at least once a day would not be there. All he needs is a bit more good luck to see him through.

Swinging open the doors to the van his dog is always the first one in. Jumping up onto the feather duvet Jack stretches his body out full length with his hind legs characteristically, sticking out behind.

Dragging along in a cobra yoga move he pulls his whole body and back legs across the duvet until he is on his own sheep skin mat. Scratching the warm wool, he makes a little nest for himself. Following his stubby tail around and around in a tight circle he finally lays down. Reaching over the dog's head Jerry grabs the corner of an extra cover, pulling it over Jacks back, ensuring he is warm after such a wet day.

Jerry got the duvet for the van just before a trip with his little family to Tofino for winter storm watching. It was the last year he had both his wife and son by his side in the van for a whole month during summer. After that summer trip it was a struggle to get Jan to agree to much more than two or three days at a time.

The summer trip was the last time his son would even enter the van if Jerry were there. Saying he was too big for the van. Or saying the van was too small for three adults. In the end Jordan said he was not coming on the Tofino trip with his dad. And he did not.

During Jordan's teenage years, family holidays in the van left the kid with some bitter feelings about travelling with Dad. Jordan resented having to go on family trips shortly after he turned seventeen. When Jordan was smaller though; oh boy - those were the days.

Reclining in the front seat, as much as his sturdy frame would allow, Jerry looks up to the many glow in the dark stars, shining above his head. Together, mother and son placed them there, as a surprise for Jerry's birthday many years ago.

Every night after all the other lights are out, for about ten minutes, the stars glow bright over his head; one heck of a happy memory for Jerry. Never understanding, how it seems so indicative of human nature to grab hold of pain and suffering, as if to do so were a life raft.

Jerry's preference is to grab onto the brass ring each time it passes his way. And that is what these memories, as they resurface over and over, are for him. Laying beneath the glow in the dark stars is one more chance to grab the brass ring and have a moment of happiness; until the memory fades and reality has its way of sinking back in. He is alone and will live out the rest of his life alone. Except for Jack that is.

CHAPTER THREE

Another Monday and a routine Mavis is beginning to dread. She has finished putting together a collection of food dishes that will make up tonight's dinner. If she hurries, she can get to their place on time. Mavis's neighbour told her yesterday while leaning over the back fence, and not for the first time either, that Mavis spoils her kids.

"Why don't they at least pick you up Mavis? Or here is an idea, meet you at the sky train? Why not eh Mavis? Or, I have another idea; why not invite them to your place for a change. Here you are cooking like a demon...every week. Well – you are a good mother - that's what you are.

"What meal do you have planned this time?" The neighbour always asks the very same question every single week "What is it you're cooking up today?" And every week Mavis makes something a little bit different. No duplicates inside of a calendar month; they would not like that.

She has wondered if any of them would notice if she did make the same thing twice in a row. If it is something, they all liked they might not complain too much. In the beginning, Mavis loved helping in this way.

Her daughter Doreen went back to work full-time a couple of years ago when she thought the twin boys were old enough. Doreen works as a chicken catcher of all things, on and off since her first husband, Raymond, left and took their son Geoffrey with him. When her second child, Charlene, was born she continued work on a part time basis; mostly weekends if she could make it.

Mavis could never imagine why they kept taking her back, but Doreen was one of their best workers. She even got an award as employee of the month a few times a year. She complained so much about Mondays and feeding the kids and her husband; and Mavis - well Mavis felt needed now. A highlight would have been if her oldest grandchild, Geoffrey, would be there too occasionally.

He is rarely there and never for dinner on Mondays. In fact, Geoffrey visits his mother as seldom as possible. Never specifically to see her; but he goes about once a month or so to take his younger sister Charlene out.

They go for lunch or coffee and sometimes a walk. At least one time in the last six months, they went to a movie. Geoffrey spends as little time as he can in his mother's presence and as far as Mavis knows, he never seeks out Doreen's company just the two of them.

When Mavis goes to Doreen's on Monday's she takes enough food for an extra night. Then Doreen can have a break on Tuesday or Wednesday too if she is smart. Mavis loves leftovers.

Besides making plenty for all of them, she makes enough for her own dinner Tuesday night. By the time Tuesday rolls around Mavis is quite tired from all the cooking and travelling by bus the day before. And the welcome of leftovers on her refrigerator shelves cannot be measured.

Last week when she arrived at her daughter's place, she found the leftover meal she had put lovingly there the week before still in the fridge. What a waste. She is noticing this happens quite often.

Mavis prides herself on not judging others, but the wastefulness is getting under her skin. Mavis often marvels to herself about their frequent claims of fatigue and poverty. And only once in a blue moon do, they show any kind of thankfulness or gratitude for the homemade meals.

Doreen usually makes something like hot dogs or macaroni dinner from a box, or her favourite - frozen pizza. Or worse, she takes her hard-earned money and orders from a restaurant. There is an expression Mavis likes to think of as one of her many personal credos – When you judge someone it does not define who they are, it defines who you are.

If she avoids judgment then no one including and especially Mavis herself, will know how she really feels about the way her children live. Impulsively Mavis decides not to bring enough food for tomorrow too. Just tonight's dinner this time. Very carefully, she unpacks all the food right down to the bottom of her new oversize plaid shopping cart.

With the food laid neatly out on the counter, she starts to estimate how much is needed for tonight's dinner. Pleased with herself she realizes she has enough left over for several meals to have here at home if she put them into aluminum TV dinner trays saved many years before.

The compartmentalized TV dinner trays remind her of when she first met her late husband, Stan. A lifelong bachelor he bought TV dinners for himself and these were some of the same saved up trays. Relics they were of a long-gone day. Once Stan met Mavis, he never bought another TV dinner. But Mavis still used the saved-up containers for occasions such as this.

Getting right down to work she manages to package six dinners for her own self to put in the freezer. If she does this every week, she will not have to cook at all for herself. On second thought taking the dinners back out of the freezer, she places five of them in the bottom of her cart. She can freeze them at Doreen's.

Feeling satisfied with her decision Mavis repacks her plaid cart. Glancing at the clock on the wall above the fridge she sees its already past time to get ready to go. She has a few minutes to wash, put on a fresh skirt, dab a bit of lipstick on her pale lips and get out the door if she wants to be there a bit early.

Mavis tries to get to her daughter's place before anyone else is home. This gives her a chance to clean the house up a bit before setting the table and putting the dinner in to warm. Everything needs to be ready and waiting when the family arrives home.

The two younger kids stay with the neighbour lady, Ricki, on Mondays and Tuesdays. Doreen's daughter, Charlene, looks after her two little brothers and Ricki's kids after school on Thursday and Friday. It is a good arrangement; one that saves both households money.

Mavis offered to look after the little ones, but Doreen said no, "They would rather be with their friends." Just as well, Mavis found the three to be holy terrors. Well the seven-year-old twins were holy terrors for sure and their older sister ... well she was a sultry teen with a growing look of double trouble in her eye and little to say to her grandmother these days.

Mavis supposed the attitudes picked up in early childhood were carried forth and magnified in adolescence. In many ways Mavis is beginning to see how the sixteen-year-old Charlene is showing signs of taking after Doreen. And Doreen took her cue directly from her own father.

Robin sent Mavis right back to work in the office at Woolworths, within weeks of each of her daughter's births. Robin worked afternoons so he was the main child minder during the day until the girls had both started schools. But by that time all the damage Robin could do, had been done.

When Doreen's daughter Charlene was born, things went well for the first few years. Who knows, maybe Doreen saw baby Charlene as her second chance to be a good mother. But as time marched on, Doreen began marching to the liquor outlet as soon as Charlene's dad left for work. By the time Charlene was five, the police had been around because one of the neighbours reported Doreen had sent the kid to buy smokes off the fence living in the complex.

The fence was called Dump Truck because he would sell any hot item, he could get his hands on. He once joked with a security guard that an item he was selling had fallen right out the back of a dump truck that was going by. Dump Truck was long gone now.

But guys like him get replaced and this time it was Roxie and Ray who could be counted on to sell a single cigarette for a fortune. But their ethics usually dictated not to sell to kids.

Years before Roxie and Ray came along with their more ethical practices; Doreen would send Charlene off to Dump Truck to buy a couple of ciggies when she had smoked all she had before hubby got home. And a bottle of beer for hubby too so he did not blow his gasket that there was no dinner to be had. Ronny was a good cook though, so food was always on the table for his little girl Charlene.

It was after Charlene started kindergarten when the real

trouble gained speed. Doreen went back to her old ways of boozing it up or getting stoned in the daytime. Invariably she would eventually try to trade sex for booze and cigarettes from Dump Truck. These are things Mavis and Doreen's oldest son Geoffrey, do not know. Doreen made up her own version of events putting herself in the best possible victims shining light.

So, misunderstood. She was a lonely housewife who innocently invited a friend in, only to be taken advantage of. Once again Doreen had been found passed out drunk in the marital bed with her spandex pants down around her ankles and a carton of cigarettes on her chest. The sticky note attached said, – last freebie Doreen, next time you pay with cash. And it was signed Dump Truck. Charlene's dad left for good that time. The twins were born a few years later.

Their life was so different than their older brother, Geoffrey's. Geoffrey took after his father and had the advantage of being raised by a surprisingly good guy. And Mavis supposed she never took the time to get know any of the other dads properly. Well except for once a week when she saw Keith, the twin's father, and Doreen's pretend husband. Mavis reminds herself not to judge Doreen's lifestyle choices.

Mavis's own choices had not been stellar either. Her choice in a husband and father for her children, for example, had not been a good one. She was happily swept away by the attention he paid her. Attention coming out of nowhere.

Her future husband had been relentless in his pursuit. Mavis by that time, had given up entirely on herself as a person of interest to the opposite sex. With her looks and lack of impressive job, or personal style she felt her prospects as a wife and mother were hopeless.

Just a few weeks out of high school, the shy and drab Mavis, already knew she was no match for the trend setters of the world. She took a job at Woolworths in the office and there she stayed until she met the man of her dreams.

She still recalls the day she met Robin. An odd and beautiful name for a man. Or so she thought at the time. And it was love at first sight when she heard his name. And his voice; smooth and sexy - like a movie star...

The day he came into the Woolworths store, he made a bee line straight for her. Mavis usually worked in the back-room or in the office where she was learning to do the books. But on the day Robin came in, she felt as if fate was calling her name. One of the pretty young girls her boss liked to keep up front, was off sick.

Mavis was the only one available, so there she was, ready to see to customers. It was Robin she saw that day and back he came several times throughout that first week to see her. Then day after day, month after month, one of her work mates would come fetch her from the stockroom saying in a sing song voice, "Robin's here."

She loved the sound of Robin said aloud. When she heard someone else say his name her whole body filled with pride that she had caught his heart. And more than a few times, she got cuffed across the mouth for calling him Robin when they were out in public or when he was on the way out with his pals.

Once, the minute they returned home after a party he said her name, "Mavis." When she turned - one smack right in the face led to more. She forgave him though. He was drunk.

The next morning his big blue, red tinged eyes looking

sad and weepy as he held her close. Then forcing reluctant legs apart so he could show her how sorry he was. Another time was a whole week after she had called him Robin in front of his boss.

And that time was the worst because she lost her first baby after she got punched repeatedly in the stomach...with Robin chanting with each punch "Never call me Robin... Never call me Robin..." Robin was simply Rob, to all who knew him. Mavis thought calling him Robin would soften the walls her husband built up around himself.

Both Doreen and Bethany took after their dad. They had truly little of Mavis in either looks or temperament. Bethany had her father's work ethic though. And his temper; both had that. And both had his love of alcohol or some other mood-altering substance.

Poor Doreen had her troubles with both drugs and booze. That is how she lost Geoffrey, well lost custody at any rate. Geoffrey was better off with his dad but he was still loyal enough to Doreen that he gave her a call or took a moment to say hello, when he picked his sister up.

Bethany had no kids, thank god. But she did like them enough, or so she would have anyone believe. And she liked time off and travelling too, so Bethany chose to be a teacher. The best of both worlds she said. Mavis did not see it. Her liking kids that is. She spoke of her students and their parents and her colleagues as if she truly hated them.

Bethany seemed like she just put in time until summer or spring break rolled around then she would take one of her girlfriends on a trip somewhere festive. Both girls had their dads impossibly blue eyes and sexy good looks. And both had that low seductive, sexy voice, which tended to fool people into believing they were something they were not.

Bethany for example drew men to her like a magnet; it was women she liked, not men. And like their dad both daughters started to gain a big pot belly by the time they hit their thirty fifth birthday. In Doreen's defence she might have gained a bit more weight than Bethany because of all the pregnancies.

WHEN MAVIS GOT off the sky train, she had one more bus to catch, then she would be at Doreen's. She held that place of Doreen's in disdain. The whole complex of town homes was overrun with screaming, dirty kids and ethnicities of every sort and lay about men.

The immigrants were not the problem though as far as Mavis was concerned. And if they ever became a problem it was because of the poor example held up for them by people like her pretend son in law Keith and even her own daughter, Doreen.

Most of the immigrants were brand new to Canada; some with refugee status. They were good honest people just trying to get jobs and make a better life for their families. Mavis felt sure the only reason Keith was never there on Monday when she arrived was, he wanted her to think he had an honest job too.

And Mavis being Mavis, went along with the charade. Even telling her neighbour that very morning about how hard Keith worked. Never once mentioning she was quite sure his job involved something the other side of legal.

The one time she saw Keith look like he was at work he was passing off some containers from the back of his truck to the cons who managed the complex next to Doreen's. Keith kept looking over his shoulder until Roxie passed him some cash. Then he got out of there fast.

Keith was seen by Mavis one other time trying it on with Roxie's daughter. She was a girl just a few years older than Charlene. She had gone through a rough patch with drugs but was on the straight and narrow at that time. Mavis interrupted Keith before he could do real damage. But he kept his distance ever since, and when she did see him, she kept her lip zipped and pretended all was well.

No, Mavis always tried to paint the best picture of her kids, their current partners, and her grand kids. Mavis tried to paint a bright picture of anyone she met. These were all the thoughts that occupy the mind of Mavis as she travels by bus, rapid transit then buses again before she gets to her daughter's. When she finally arrives at Doreen's unit Mavis can see down the stairwell to the basement door; it has been kicked in.

Not sure what to do about it she goes to Ricki's place next door. She can hear the muted sound of kids and TV and the sound of a one-sided telephone conversation. After quietly knocking and waiting for an answer Mavis carefully slides the glass doors open a crack and peeks in to see Ricki not four feet away.

Ricki had seen Mavis and her plaid cart go by outside but does not hear the timid knock. When Mavis slides the door open Ricki waves Mavis through. Stepping into the kitchen Mavis is surprised and impressed with everything looking as neat as a pin and she smells the scent of a stew or something on the stove.

Ricki says her goodbyes into the phone and greets Mavis, saying she does not think Doreen is home yet. "Well Ricki, I'm sorry to trouble you but, I should call the building manager if you have the number because the backdoor at Doreen's place is kicked in."

"What do you mean the backdoor; do you mean the glass door?" Mavis is looking around not really listening; she is getting tired and a bit distressed by the damage to the door. "Come on Mavis, why don't you just show me?"

Ricki is out her door like a shot heading to her pal Doreen's place. Right away she sees what Mavis means and leans in to ring the bell beside the sliding doors. Turning her head toward Mavis she says in a loud voice, "If anyone is in there, this'll make them just piss right off! Whoops sorry about the language, did not mean to say that. Come on, give me your key; let's go in."

Mavis acts braver than she feels stepping through the open sliding door. Ricki goes to check the place out and tells Mavis to give Doreen a call at work. Doreen though, had never given her mother the direct number to the place she worked, saying she would not need it. Mavis always takes no for an answer. Instead she calls Doreen on her cell phone.

Doreen answers with, "What the fuck are you calling me on my cell for?" Doreen offers no hello mum or how are you mum or is everything ok? Nope, just the grief; Mavis quietly and calmly outlines what is going on before handing the phone over to Ricki. The first thing Ricki does is turn her back on Mavis and cover the mouthpiece so Mavis cannot hear either end of the story.

Before handing the phone back to Mavis, Ricki presses the speaker button so they could have a three-way conversation. But the first words Ricki hears out of Doreen's mouth are, "Are you some sort of a mental moron Mother? What the friggin hell! Why would you get Ricki of all people...?"

Ricki snatches the phone away from a trembling Mavis, throws her arm across her shoulder and shouts into the phone "Watch your mouth! Do not ever speak to your mother like that again! You are the mental moron Doreen. What the heck, for Christ sake?"

Flipping the older model cell phone closed she draws Mavis in and gives her a hug; a very tight, strong hug. The kind her second husband Stan was known for. Mavis feels a heat on her face.

Realizing its tears, in her embarrassment she makes to pull away until she sees, it is Ricki who weeps. "My mum died." Is all she says, just that. Letting go of Mavis, Ricki tells her she is going home to make sure the kids are all settled and fine then she will be right back. They would have a coffee or something together.

Not missing a beat or giving in to the self-pity and humiliation Mavis feels she puts the kettle on to boil and begins to unpack the dinner. Ricki's a bit longer than a few minutes and when she returns Mavis smells the familiar aroma of cannabis.

Do not judge, Mavis mentally admonishes herself and instead thinks about the package of bakery made Nanaimo bars she brought along. Placing a few slices onto a plate, Mavis pours them both a cup of coffee and there they sit, each deep in her own thoughts: companionably silent.

The Nanaimo bars get swallowed up amazingly fast and when they are gone Ricki turns to Mavis and says, "Please don't let her talk to you like that Mavis. You are not doing her any favours you know? She does not know how to be. She blames her dad, and she blames you too. For how she is I mean. Like how she treats people."

Mavis hangs her head. Blame was the last thing she expected. Never a cross word or an angry hand had she ever risen to either of her daughters. She does not know what to say, how to defend herself, or even if she should.

"Don't get me wrong Mavis. I know you would not hurt a

fly. But that is the problem; you never stood up for yourself with anyone. Doreen claims she does not either. But she says her dad was always putting you down; and you just let him. Is that right Mavis? Did you?"

Nodding yes is all Mavis can manage. She is as close to tears as she has been in a long time. Unsure of what she is feeling, she stays quiet for fear she will say the wrong thing. Putting her hand on the table to stop it from shaking, Ricki leans over and puts both her own hands around Mavis's one. Mavis feels warm and cared for.

"I'll tell you what Mavis. You come knock on my door again next week and we can have another little chat. OK? But right now, I gotta get back to the kiddies. OK Hun?" Abruptly Ricki let go of Mavis's hand; she heads toward the door saying a simple "Bye."

As Ricki slips out the sliding glass doors, she does not cast a backward glance Mavis's way. Mavis understands why Ricki makes such an awkward exit. It could not have been easy to tell Mavis it was her daughter Doreen who kicked the basement door open two days before when one of the boys locked her out for the fun of it. Or that Doreen does not want to call the building managers because in the end the maintenance department will send her a bill for a new door.

DINNER IS much quieter than the usual Monday. Doreen is almost polite to her mother. Polite is not the right word – contrite is the word, Mavis imagines. Having your best friend witness those unforgivable words must be hard to take. The kids are really put out there is no after dinner sweet to take upstairs to their rooms with them.

One by one they leave the table not saying thanks for dinner or even goodbye to their grandmother. As usual when it is time to leave the three adults go through the routine of Keith saying, "Hey, why not let me drive you tonight." And both Doreen and Mavis telling him at the same time, "No, you're over the limit."

Just before she leaves and as she packs up her empty containers Mavis swings open the deep freeze. Pointing happily, she says, "Oh Doreen – I almost forgot. I left some TV dinner trays for you. I made them up before I came. It's just the same as we had for dinner tonight, nothing fancy."

For answer, Doreen slams the freezer shut. Then grabs it open again, hauling out the trays and stuffs them haphazardly in her mother's tartan bag.

"Are you out your f'ing mind! Why would I want TV dinners in aluminum foil? They are not even microwave safe and besides - aluminum is bad for you! What are you trying to do? Kill us all... Hey? Why do you do these things anyway? Go home Mum. I know you mean well but for Christ sake. Think about it!"

Mavis scurries to the door. Dragging her cart behind her; she says not one word, she just hurries away off into the rain. She makes it to the bus stop just in time to see the bus pulling away. Mavis stands next to the wet bench to wait for another bus to come. The silent mantra of - if you miss one bus, the next one will be along... ringing in her head.

Ricki was right; she ought not to let Doreen speak to her like that. She should stand up for herself. She wonders if the recreation centre has an assertiveness training course or if those classes are still in vogue. She is just thinking that she missed the boat on learning how to assert herself when the next bus does come along.

THE RIDE HOME is quicker tonight. It is recounting her blessings of the day that makes the trip speed by. She thinks of Ricki and her kindness, her warm embrace. She thinks of the little white dog that jumped on her in the afternoon.

Sitting on a seat with the other sky train passengers, Mavis spins the story of the little white dog into a sparkling vista of happy endings off in the distant future. Whiling away the ride home she weaves the memory of the dog out to include a friendship with the man who called the dog Jack.

In her daydream she is friends with both the little white dog and the man with the sad blue eyes and white wavy hair. She will give him an aluminum tray or two filled with TV dinners next time they meet...

Pretty soon she is at the end of the line. Waking up from her reverie, she feels the sharp nudge of the next load of passengers trying to find a seat; Standing she gets ready to disembark.

WHEN THE BUS pulled away earlier in the day from the Mt. Pleasant stop, near where Mavis got her bakery treats, her eyes followed back along the sidewalk. Watching with curiosity out of the corner of her eye as the little dog skipped beside the white-haired man.

Marching together through the rain Mavis's heart goes out to them both on such a cold and wet day. This is not the first time she has seen them together and it is not the first time she has seen that dog either. But this time she is sure she had met the dog before.

Mavis is certain the little dog, the man had called Jack, once belonged to someone on her street. Turning to face forward on the bus she feels a thrill of flattery that the little dog, recognized her.

Brushing the hem of her skirt she straightens the edge, so it lays flat against her knee. She carefully arranges her decade's old London Fog raincoat, so it does not get a crease. Deep in thought she recalls a day she found a little white dog in her lane. He was just sitting there looking up at her gate when she went to take out the weekly garbage for pickup.

That would have been one or so years ago. She invited him into the yard then shut the gate and did a bit of gardening, watching him all the while out of the corner of her eye. He found an old tennis ball under a bush then brought it over and for a few minutes they played fetch together.

First things first though, into the house they went so she could get her glasses to read his name tag, then she dialled what she presumed was the owner's number. When a message machine picked up, she left her information, "Hello my name is Mavis Everly, I just found a little white dog wandering in my lane. There is no name on the tag.... just this number. Shall I call you back?"

Then she hung up without leaving her number. A part of her hoped they would not have the presence of mind to press *69 or more likely look at their call display to name who she was. Another more real part said, do not ever give out your personal information and phone number to strangers. But she just had, had she not? She left her name; very foolish of her.

Turning from the phone she almost tripped over the little dog. There he sat, looking up at her. With tilted head and exaggerated slowness, he moved it side to side as if trying to see inside her mind and read it. When their eyes met, he grinned showing her a set of white teeth. Very comical. She laughed and laughed so hard; tears began to stream down her cheeks as her heart burst with the sheer pleasure of the moment.

Bending at the waist she reached down for the little dog, bringing him up to her chest to hold him close. She felt a calm settle over her making her feel so relaxed that she wished she had gotten a little dog of her own, but she supposed it was too late now.

Carrying him into her bathroom with her, she pulled open a cabinet drawer with one hand and held him tight with the other. Taking out an old hairbrush she raised it to his back cautious of an angry reaction. She had little knowledge of dogs except to know some did not like to be brushed.

This one did it appeared. In fact, once she got started, he loved it, making soft groaning sounds of pleasure when she ran the brush down his back. Each time it reached his tail the little dog gave a shiver of what Mavis imagined as pure pleasurable delight.

Opening her fridge, she looked inside for a little doggy type snack and settled on some chicken and cheese. Chopping the cheese and chicken into small pieces she wrapped them up in wax paper and put them in the pocket of her cardigan. Together they went into the yard for her to do some more gardening. The sky though had gone from overcast to brilliant sun.

Instead of pulling weeds in the heat Mavis decided to enjoy the day by bringing the dog up onto her lap. There they sat for an hour or so until she heard the ring of her phone inside the house. Not bothering to make a run for it, Mavis continues to enjoy her day a while longer. Handing over the last bits of chicken and cheese she settled her little friend on the ground and went in to hear a message. With a dim hope, she wished there were not one.

The caller left their number and wanted her to call back. "That's my parent's dog." That was the message. Before she could give it further thought Mavis had picked up the phone and dialled. She realized right away that the person who picked up did not use English as a first language.

She was just trying to figure out what language she might be hearing when the phone obviously changed hands and the voice from the answering machine came on. Again, she was told, "That is my parent's dog. How did you get it?" It thought Mavis. It is, he, with a name presumably.

In the background almost drowning out the speaker's voice on the other end of the line, Mavis heard two people speaking rapidly in what she now presumed to be Chinese or Cantonese; she could not tell the difference.

OK, now she knew who owned the dog. It was the people in the new house down the street. She might have seen the dog on the window-ledge of their car as it drove by. Her mind drifting, she was brought back to attention by the girl asking, "What's your address. I'm coming to get him right now."

CHAPTER FOUR

A month after Mavis had her chance meeting with Jerry, she decides the time has come for a fresh look. Returning from her weekly hair appointment, she keeps catching sight of herself in store windows on the way home. The mirror in her small entry gives her a full view of what she has done. It is a shock; a thrill to see how she looks.

Hair that for the first time in her life, looks a bit stylish. She asked her hairdresser, Owen, to do what he had wanted to do for years. In the mirror someone new is returning her gaze. Turning her head side to side she gives an inward nod. "Yes!" Said aloud, "this will do just fine."

Her driver's license is ready to expire and though she rarely drives she keeps her license for ID. She now has a new look for her photo. Lifting the glasses that hang on a brand-new chain around her neck, she holds them up to get a better look. Gone are the dark brown, neat rows of tight sausage roll shaped curls she had worn forever.

Replaced by and completely stripped of colour, this latest look is short and sleek. Her hair looks like a seal she thinks. Owen called it a bob; ash grey, he called her enhanced hair colour. "Grey is the new blond. Mavis honey you look gorgeous," Owen said. The soft grey, such a shock with her very dark brown eyes and still very dark brown thick eyebrows. She kept her hair so dark because of those heavy dark eyebrows.

Owen called her brows sexy; said to never pluck them. "They are perfect." Owen promised instead of coming for a weekly shampoo and curl she could come for a wash and blow dry until she got the hang of doing it on her own. And Owen wanted her to change the day she came in from her usual Wednesday morning to early Monday instead. Telling her, she would look good for Monday's when she caught the bus to Doreen's. Owen has never met Doreen but has a sneaking suspicion Doreen was not as nice as Mavis.

THE NEXT TWO Mondays following the one Ricki had consoled her on; she had seen the little dog Jack again on her way to Surrey. She is sure Jack's human friend is waiting for her with Jack in tow sporting a brand-new leash and warm looking raincoat. Jack's human friend is called Jerry. Jack and Jerry; cute.

Mavis and Jerry chatted long enough that she missed her bus. And then she missed the next one too and soon it seemed pointless to go all the way to Doreen's.

At the end of their visit on that first day while they sat and talked Mavis reached in her bag taking out a glass dish filled with cabbage rolls. With a warm smile on her face and in her heart, she offered them to Jerry. Asking, "Shall we meet next week; you can return the dish then? I will come two hours earlier though in case we want a nice chat before I go to the sky train. I hope we do." And on her way back home, she fantasizes about Mavis, Jack, and Jerry. They would be a happy little family.

ON THE PHONE later that day, Doreen does not care if her mother misses a week or two. In fact, it is a bit of a surprise her mother keeps coming back; but does not say so to Mavis. It is not as if Doreen has a conscience about her treatment of her mother. Though she sometimes wonders what motivates her to be so mean to her in the first place.

Doreen always gives in to impulses; she tells herself she cannot help it. Her mother had long been anyone's doormat; someone easy to push around. Mavis being Mavis, she just begged to be a perfect target as far as Doreen is concerned.

When Ricki came to talk to Doreen about what happened the last time Mavis brought dinner over, she told Doreen what she thought. She said, Doreen pushed Mavis around because it gave her a feeling of power and control; in at least one part of her life. Ricki said Doreen's relationships were all falling apart, and she said Doreen felt an urgent need to have power and control over something or someone.

Doreen though; she thought Ricki was no shrink and should keep her pop psychology to herself. Just because Ricki was going to school and taking all those self-help and aptitude tests did not make her a relationship expert. In Doreen's opinion Ricki was becoming a know it all.

MAVIS AND JERRY see each other during her two-week break from going to Surrey. The food she would normally take to Doreen's she makes up for Jerry instead. He is thrilled by the kindness. And thrilled a second time when Mavis reaches up to pat his clean-shaven cheek.

Turning his face in time, he plants a light kiss right in the middle of the palm of her hand. Blushing brightly Mavis waved her goodbyes and got on her bus.

When Mavis arrives back to Doreen's after a two-week break, the kids at least, seem a bit glad to see her. They got used to having a nice homemade dinner once a week. Ricki sees her coming and rounds up all the children to join Mavis in Doreen's kitchen for a chat. Clamouring around the table as Ricki and Mavis try to have their promised visit, the twins are anxious to know about the dessert.

It is Mavis's habit to stop at a bakery in Mt Pleasant on her way to Surrey. It is not because Mavis does not bake; it's because the bakery called, Gitta's Sweets and Deli, was a favourite of Doreen's. Finding pleasure in seeing the shop logo on the sweets box is a throwback to Doreen's childhood.

Every Saturday Robin had taken both girls there for a bowl of borscht and a treat. Mavis stayed home to do the week's housework and laundry on her day off. And it was later discovered Robin left the girls to their sweet treat while he took his own treat with Gitta in the back room for five minutes.

Gitta still owns the bakery and it is with gratitude that Mavis greets her behind the counter each Monday. The day Mavis left Robin taking the girls with her, it was Gitta who gave her money and a phone number where she would find help and safety. And as far as Mavis is aware, it is Gitta who kept Robin's mind and body occupied while he got over his family leaving. And it was Gitta who took his mind off the idea of dragging them back home.

CHARLENE IS SEEN through the sliding glass door with an arm load of books. Ricki jumps from her seat to greet her and Mavis watches Ricki pass Charlene a house key then hears her say, "...then come back here and say a proper hello to your Gran before you hit those books." Ricki faces Mavis with a conspiratorial look in her eyes. She says, "Charlene does her homework, and she studies at my place every day...or most days. She is a smart kid Mavis. I try to help her out, just with a quiet spot and a bit of encouragement that is all... but don't tell Doreen. She'd flip."

Mavis isn't about to question why Doreen will flip. Doreen flips over anything or anyone she feels inferior to or jealous of. She never attained her own education easily or without help. She may not have finished school without a bit of help right down to Mavis or young Bethany writing high school essays and finishing assignments for her.

It was not Doreen manipulating anyone; it was Doreen not having the articulation to form proper written sentences or well-structured paragraphs. These days Doreen would have been considered to have a learning disability. Mavis supposed she had let Doreen down. Not doing her any favours as Ricki had said two weeks ago. A good mother would have found a way for Doreen to succeed on her own without having to reach beyond her skill set.

MAVIS SNAPS out of thoughts of Monday and the visit to Surrey; she feels someone looking at her. Geoffrey: with hands cupped around his face squinting through the glass of her window.

Opening the door wide she says, "what a welcome surprise!" Throwing her arms around his neck in an uncharacteristic spontaneous show of affection, gives Geoffrey a bit of a jolt. His Gran looks and is acting unlike herself.

"I'm the one surprised! What have you done with my Gran?" Geoffrey does not know what to think of this transformation. Every time he comes to visit his Gran at her lane way house, he knows this accommodation is so much better for Mavis than it would have been for him.

With rent from the big house, she can put a bit aside for other repairs that the house needs. A few weeks ago, she showed him plans she had drawn up to revamp the unused suite in the basement of the main house.

Today she tells him she hopes his sister, Charlene might be able to go to university and if so, she could have somewhere nice to live. Remembering what he had seen as he watched her through the window as she preened in front of the mirror he wonders if her next momentous change will be to upgrade her wardrobe.

On second thought her pleated skirts, coloured tights and practical black shoes looked quite trendy or at least she looks intentional with the new haircut and colour. And of course, she would dress this way; it has always been her style never changing since she was a teenager. As far as he knows.

Giving her shoulder a sideways hug, Geoffrey pulls out a chair and asks if soups on yet. It is Wednesday and that means two things, a weekly trip to get her hair done and soup.

Geoffrey's habit is to stop off at his gran's every Wednesday or so to have some lunch. In the old days he also would change a light bulb or move furniture, anything she needed. Now the tenants looked after the house and yard, and her little postage stamp sized lawn too giving it a weed whack each week. When she needed a repair for the house, it was covered by the rent.

His grandpa Stan had left her in good financial shape. Some sort of investment had matured last year, and she used it to build her little laneway house and there was enough left over to attend to fixing up the suite and a few other things she had in mind.

While the soup is warming Mavis throws a batch of biscuits in the oven; Geoffrey leans against the counter talking away about his plans. Mavis is barely listening to what he says. For once her mind is on her own prospects.

She half listens while he tells her about the small second-hand Smart car he just bought; telling her it needs repairs, and it will be awhile before she can have her own vehicle back.

But as her mind wanders, she completely misses what Geoffrey is saying about being accepted at UBC to do a PhD program and his acceptance as a TA, which is the first step to teaching. She never got the details right anyway.

When people ask what Geoffrey does, she says, "Full time student, part time advocate and part time computer geek." But when she says it, she has no idea what he does. All she knows for sure is, she is immensely proud of him, no matter what.

Graduating two years ahead of his peers, he got a full scholarship for his first degree which he got in record time. Then he got the job at the university library and sometimes he was on loan to other libraries around the city. He had been doing it for so long Mavis felt too embarrassed to suddenly ask, "What do you do again?" She knows his big plan is to teach library and computer sciences at the university level. He is only 23; he has lots of time.

And as far as Mavis is concerned at his age, he is too young to live with a woman. Not in maturity though. Mavis always felt Geoffrey was one of those young fellows that would always seem old. Geoffrey was like no one in the family at all. Not like her side of the family and not like his dad's side of the family.

In fact, the only person Geoffrey shared similarities to seemed to be Mavis's second husband Stan. When Geoffrey was a little guy, after he had gone to live with his dad, Mavis and Stan looked after Geoffrey while his dad was at work. Geoffrey followed Stan around like Stan was his idol calling him, "Pop." And little Geoffrey picked up a thing or two. Catching sight of her own reflection in the window above the sink she turned to Geoffrey and said apropos of nothing either of them had been talking about, "You have my eyes."

Geoffrey just stared at her. He is realizing that for some reason today his Gran is in a world all her own. Smiling he kisses the top of her head, "You look great Gran, it's taken me a few minutes to decide but I like your hair like this. Good move. And yes - I got your eyes and eyebrows!"

This made her smile, and she began to tell a long story about a dog she had rescued the year before. Geoffrey remembers the day because she talked about that dog for months. She worried - were those people taking good enough care of him.

But right now, it was his turn to have a wandering mind as she chattered happily on. Glad she was feeling so good. He is not about to mention his mum asked him to talk to Mavis about something that happened two weeks before. Something, Doreen hinted Mavis had done that may have caused a falling out.

Mavis had not turned up at Doreen's the last two weeks and this week when she came, she seemed unfriendly and distant. Apparently only bringing enough food for one meal...

His guess is Gran has forgotten all about his mother and her screaming fits of rage. What else can you do? Geoffrey knows his Gran and knows by next week she will be back in the groove of her usual routine of putting on a good act around Doreen.

ON HIS WAY to the library he is scheduled to work at, he picks up a newspaper and just for fun looks for VW Vans. A 1965 Classic with pop up roof is what he is after. It was Grandpa Stan, who had shown him the first one. They were at BC Place checking out an RV and boat show. Stan got car sick on long rides, but said he would have loved to get Mavis a VW Van to drive around in.

"Can't you just see her Geoffrey, sitting behind the wheel and then hopping up to pull a tray of cookies out of thin air? I can see her putting the bed down to stretch out and read on a wet day and listen to the tapping of raindrops falling on the roof at the same time."

They laughed together at the thought. Geoffrey never forgot that day or any other day he spent with Stan. Stan was his hero. Stan was the only granddad Geoffrey ever knew. His dad's father had gone AWOL when Raymond was born.

His Gran would not let her ex, Robin, anywhere near Geoffrey once he left the care of Doreen. Then of course Robin lost interest anyway. Robin lost interest in most things unless there was going to be some personal pay off for him.

Geoffrey's mother Doreen, lost interest in him too after he went to live with his dad when he was two. His parents had been kids themselves when he was born. He had to hand it to his dad for getting it together so fast to look after a baby. Raymond never remarried or even had a girlfriend after Doreen started using drugs. "Once burned, twice shy," he told Geoffrey one time.

When Geoffrey graduated from high school his dad took a small inheritance left to him by his mum and moved to Costa Rica where Raymond's aunt owned a hotel. Now that was a sad day. A day when Geoffrey realized how he had taken his dad for granted. His dad had sacrificed having a full life to look after a kid when he was a kid himself.

Getting ready to go Geoffrey gets up and puts all their dishes in the dish washer. Teasingly he tells Mavis he wants to move into her laneway house after all.

Not missing a beat his Gran gives a thoughtful squint then says, "Leave it with me Geoffrey, I can work something out." As cool as she looks with her new hairdo, you would never know the kind of life his Gran once lived.

There was a time in the distant past that she and her two kids took refuge from a violent husband in a woman's shelter. To hear his mother, Doreen, tell the tale you would think it was a case of child abduction and the man left behind was a harmless hero. His grandmother never said a bad word about anyone, especially her children's father.

In recent days Geoffrey visited Robin for the first time - just the two of them; and a vastly different picture emerged. Robin or Rob, as he insisted Geoffrey call him had type-two diabetes and was confined to a wheelchair after a recent double amputation from the knee down.

He told Geoffrey how surprised he was that Mavis had let him out of her sight long enough to see him at all. Doreen came to visit every few weeks and had done so behind her mother's back from the first.

He was honest about how he treated his wife. With bragging satisfaction, he justified his every slap. Did he ever slap his kids? "No God Dam it, I'd never strike a child! Did she say I did?" Geoffrey told him to calm down and said his Gran never mentioned him at all.

Robin asked if Mavis was still married, "...to that ugly old rich guy," is how he said it. Geoffrey decided to get out of there.

Without a word he stood up and left the room. His mother was in the hall giving them privacy. Doreen was ever so grateful to Geoffrey for finally agreeing to see her old man in the hospital. He would not be going back, once was more than enough.

ON THE ROAD again after his lunch with Gran he circles her older SUV around the block a few times before he finds a spot. Usually luck is on his side and he finds a space right outside the front doors of any place he is going. But today he is distracted by how much his grandmothers changed. It feels like overnight.

Just up ahead a big truck pulls away from the curb and an old VW Van pulls right in. "Wow," says Geoffrey aloud in his car. When he gets out to plug the meter, he sees the driver emerge and is surprised it is an older man he is seen around, whom he thought of as homeless.

The old guy comes into the various libraries around town and spends the allotted two hours on a computer; then he cruises through the library stacks selecting a pile of books.

Geoffrey never saw the titles but one of the librarians mentioned he had very eclectic taste. She thought he was researching some sort of cancer or all kinds of cancer. "Maybe he's looking for a cure?" was Geoffrey's reply. This old guy had been seen at the hospital library too. Who knows maybe he is, doing research on cancer?

Later Geoffrey goes to the library washroom, he bumps right into the older man; almost knocking him over. "Sorry about that Pops." Realizing it may seem rude to be called Pops, Geoffrey tries to save the situation by introducing himself and asking the man's name. "Just call me Pops, I actually like it." And off he strolled, into the art history isle.

For the first time Geoffrey notices a small notebook that Pops is making notes in. He makes a note rips it out then sticks the page in his shirt pocket.

Geoffrey goes back to work, but before he leaves for the day, he runs into his new friend again. This time they are both outside going to their vehicles. Pops gets to his first, letting a small dog wearing a sweater out. It is so he can relieve himself against a tree and do nothing else because the dog hops right back into the open door of the van. "Hey Pops. I like your Van. Is it a '65?" Surprised and smiling broadly, Pops turns toward Geoffrey asking, "Sorry, what was your name again?"

"Oh - it's Geoff... I love your van; it's the Classic '65, right? I have been trying to find one like this. I like the original colours; the yellow one especially. But really at this point I would almost go for the red or green. Yours has the original green paint job I bet? Did you paint the peace sign or buy it like this?"

Opening the front passenger door Pops motions Geoffrey over for a peek inside. The front seats are spotless. The rear of the van -not so tidy. The space is taken up with a bed laid out and crumpled bedding which the dog is completely at home on.

Catching Geoffrey's roving eye, the older man tells Geoffrey how he likes to use the van for day trips. "I put down the bed, stretch out and read all the books I take out of the library. And on fall days like this one, listening to the rain hit the roof is – well it cannot be beat.

"That is exactly what I'll be doing when I get my van!" Before parting Geoffrey says, "If you ever want to sell, I'm your man."

"There won't be a chance of that, my wife and I got this van over forty years ago. We were only the second owners. It has been parked under cover and gotten regular maintenance. It was my intention to give it to my son or even a grandchild."

Geoffrey steps back shrugging his shoulders saying, "Well I thought it would be too good to be true to find my dream, right in front of me. See you eh?" Reaching out Geoffrey shakes the other man's hand then gives a wave.

The older man gets in his van glancing for a long time in his rear-view mirror. He appears to wait until the younger man drives off. With the memory of this young guy Geoffrey calling him, Pop and then Pops, he feels choked up.

His son, Jordan, called him Pops. When he told Geoffrey to just call him Pop, he was not kidding he did like it. A familiar lump grows in his throat, his eyes burn bright with hushed tears. The emotion he feels cannot be explained but he knows its root is sorrow.

Watching Geoffrey drive off its the sorrow of knowing the young man he had the pleasure of speaking with, would never be part of his life. Knowing no young man would ever be part of his life again. And knowing he would not be coming back to this library to check out his theory; he starts up the VW.

THE NEXT STOP for Geoffrey is, 12th and Vine. His fingers are crossed that he will pick up a soccer game with some high school buddy's. Nearing the park, he sees not a soul. Turning at the next left and then left again brings him in the right direction to get him home. His Gran was right in a way; he was young to be living with a woman. He knew his Gran had been younger than him when she began her life with a partner.

He supposed you could not really call Robin much of a partner, but a husband and father; yes. Good old Robin had his way forcefully with Gran, in the storage room at Woolworths. Robin had bragged about it, "She said no, but I just went for it. I had been coming into that store for one reason only, to snag a virgin.

"Even an ugly one would put a notch on the old belt." This said that time Geoffrey went to see him in hospital, saying it, between men, conspiratorially. Locker room talk, "Then the next thing I knew - the little bitch was knocked-up. It was a shot gun wedding of course. A guy like me would never have tied the knot willingly with a plain Jane like her.

"Wouldn't you know the stupid cow lost that first baby almost right away. I should have left her then instead of waiting." Two babies came along; bang-bang, almost a year apart; all four living in a one-bedroom basement suite in her parents' house in East Van.

CHAPTER FIVE

It was the East Vancouver neighbourhood Geoffrey was heading toward right now, a block away from his great grandparent's old house. Turning into the driveway he feels lucky. The house belongs to his girlfriend and her four sisters.

Bonnie is the youngest and until the Real Estate market makes another big spike and Bonnie is finished her degree, they will keep it. Both for sentimental reasons and it provides housing for four of the girls. The one-bedroom suite he shares with Dixie is on the top floor.

There are two other one-bedroom suites in the high basement where Valerie and Lori live. And the youngest in the family, has a studio suite carved out of the main floor, made just for her. Its located in a back corner, behind the biggest suite. With three bedrooms its rent covers utilities for the sisters, taxes, and insurance.

Their oldest sister Sheri collects all five rents and pays the major bills then divvies up the change. No doubt her part is placed in some special savings account.

Dixie saves hers too. She has always shared a suite and

at one time lived on the main floor renting out the three bedrooms as shared accommodation when she was in university. She had a bed for herself on the closed-in back porch. Cramped but ultra-cool; and that's where Geoffrey spent his first night with Dixie.

They met at a university party. It was during his first year, he was a few days short of being 16. Technically he told her later; she had sex with a minor. She was finishing her master's degree in psychology at the time.

They never hooked up again until about a year ago and they had not spent a night apart since. Dixie at 32 had no delusions of why she and Geoffrey were so drawn to each other. She is a psychologist after all. Parking in the double driveway, Geoffrey looks up at the dark window of the top floor. He feels like maybe he is not joking with his Gran about living in her laneway house.

Running up three flights of stairs, on the side of the house, had lost its lustre as a means of staying fit during the past couple of weeks. He is not sure why. Dixie might say it was the change in weather; Geoffrey would say it was the change in the hours both he and Dixie kept.

JERRY IS CLOSING the big double garage doors of his laneway pad when Mrs. Bergen's niece Adele, calls out. "Jerry! May I please have a word with you?" Adele is a bit younger than Jerry but holds the ideas and values of a much older generation. He finds it humorous that Mrs. Bergen who is so young and hip in so many ways, has such a close relationship with a niece that is so old fashioned. "Adele! Have not seen you in a while. How are things?"

They exchange a few pleasantries in the lane for a few

minutes with Jack sitting calmly beside Jerry, his head swivelling back and forth. Looking from one to the other as the two human voices drone on. "Jerry, the reason I wanted to talk to you is we don't think Aunty is going to be able to manage the house any longer on her own."

Holding up her hand in a gesture that says let me finish; Adele continues with what sounds like a prepared speech. "We have a place all picked out for her in an assisted living apartment closer to where we live in Tsawwassen. I want to let you know we are planning to rent the house out. Aunty is worried about you though so I told her you can still rent the garage for your van."

Jerry is silent and grateful to Mrs. Bergen for thinking of him. Before Adele leaves, Jerry is told, in no uncertain terms he will need to find another address for his mail. "Where do you live Jerry? I hope you haven't been living in the garage for heavens sake. I think it's best if you've got another address, that you get your mail there. What do you think?"

"Oh kay. Sure, I can. I promise to put a change of address in right away. When is all this going to happen anyway? I guess I won't need to take her garbage out and mow the lawn much longer? Tell Mrs. B I'll miss her soup." Their conversation wound down quickly; what else was left to say?

JERRY SEES what is happening to the houses in his pocket of Mt. Pleasant. They are either getting torn down or major renovations are being made. One of the favourite changes is building proper laneway houses; some liked to call them carriage houses, as if they were part of a grand estate.

Closing and securing the garage door tight, Jerry gets into the front passenger side of his van. Shifting his body sideways in an old familiar way; he lets his back lean up against the passenger door with his legs stretched out across the mint condition covered and protected split bench seat; he sits in silence.

Jerry contemplates his options closing his eyes and clasping cupped hands behind his head. Jerry dreams of his son. He is fully awake but what he dreams is conjured by the question, "What if?" Fruitlessly he remains in a half-awake dream state

for an hour with the warm glow of possibility washing gently over him in waves. When his eyes eventually come open a huge sense of relief has pulled over him, like a nice warm coat.

Feeling like he had just emerged from a massage, the anger, the hurt and the worry; vanished. Taking out his journal, Jerry flicks on a reading lamp and starts writing. He writes about his son. He writes about possibility and ways to adapt to his new reality, his new life. Walking with grief or writing with grief; either way that is what Jerry is doing these days.

Today's dream is about him and Jordan giving a helping hand to Mrs. Bergen. Moving her into a senior home. The family, her family, they never helped at all. If Jordan were alive, he would be 46. Jerry's going to be 65 on his next birthday. When he did the math, he realized how young he and Jan were when they started out.

Kids these days did not seem so worldly and independent; and were they responsible? Not so much. The kid he met at the library today though; he even shook Jerry's hand. That took maturity and no doubt a good teacher guiding his development.

Speaking of teaching Jerry swings his legs out of the van and gets the dog treats with plans to put Jack through his paces. Jack's nowhere to be found. Calmly Jerry slides open the garage door just a bit and in slips Jack, as wet as a rat. "Why don't you bark?"

Gathering the wet dog up in a towel Jerry takes him over to the table. Jack shivers with all his might, trying to warm his body up. Jerry gets out an old hair dryer he once found in a garbage bin and begins to dry Jack off and warm him up at the same time. Jerry removes his new collar. It is a gift from the little lady, she said she found it, but Jerry was sure he had seen the same one in Gert's store.

"That little lady? The one who gave you the collar Jackie boy? She is a real kind-hearted chick," Jerry says aloud to Jack. Bundling Jack up in a dry blanket he carries his little buddy over to the van and lays him in his pile of lamb skin. Jack snuggles down, still shivering. "I wonder what she would make of this set up, eh Jack? Do you think she would still think you were a cute little dog?"

A week ago, and again yesterday Jerry cleaned himself up and intentionally loitered around the bus stop in hopes of spotting his new friend. Standing about 5'2" with dark horn-rimmed glasses, she was not the most fashionable lady. With the blackest, sharpest eyes Jerry had seen in a while; she seemed exactly right to him. She was old fashioned, but exactly right. Because she was kind he supposed. And kindnesses given and received are as he sees it, a way back into the world of the living.

THE LAST DAY, of the last month marked the five-year anniversary of his son's death. They were lined up to go zip lining when Jan's cell phone rang. "It's Jordan! Hang on a second Jerry...Jordan, hi Hun! What's up? Dad and I are about to go zip lining. We wish you had come with us."

Jordan was always giving them adventure gifts because otherwise they always were too busy to do fun stuff that did not involve a trip in the VW. Jerry half listened but as usual only heard a few seconds of a one-sided conversation. Pretty soon his attention drifted off to watch people zip off into the woods. The nightmare began the second he heard a gasp from Jan.

Ripping off her zip lining harness, Jan frantically insisted they leave "right now." With her back to Jerry she races away from him to find a way off the mountain, and to the rescue of her son. Turning only once to look at her husband, she blurts, "Jordan has cancer Jerry. Hurry up!"

They went straight to the hospital where the events that followed ran like a movie loop through Jerry's mind. Over and over then over again, every day. Over and over the details of a family consultation with Jordan's Doctor. Next a meeting with the hospice doctor, then researching cures. Followed by months of Jordan's treatment. His death...

Not bothering to take a leave from work, they both quit on the spot to be near their son. Only one child they had promised each other on their cross Canada trip way back when. Their love child. A baby conceived in a VW van while introducing each other to Canada and ideas of what a future would be like if spent together.

Jordan had been with them from the beginning. His conception was the start of the three of them. Without Jordan there would never have been a – them at all. Jan's parents would have made sure of that.

The van had been a gift to Jan so she could get as far away from Jerry as she could with her girlfriends. One by one the girl friends dropped out of the trip. Only Jerry remained. "Sure!" He said, "I'd love to go with you Jan, just you and me, right?"

Ben and June, still alive, rarely spoke with Jerry now. Not even when Jordan was growing up. Jan's parents did not speak to any of them. They all but ignored Jordan's funeral then a year later their own daughter's funeral. Turning up at the last minute to Jordan's saying to Jan after she gave a heart wrenching eulogy for her son, "What kind of mother doesn't even cry at her son's funeral."

Not a kind word for their loss just saying something so bizarre and untrue when they overheard them to say, "He was our son too." What had they meant? Jerry kicked story after story around in his head, like a soccer ball. He unsuccessfully tried to find a meaning of that line. Did they mean they regretted not having a son like Jordan?

The son they did have fell short. Jan's brother was a nonstarter. He was two years younger than Jan. After getting a degree in something useless, he still lived at home and never had a real job as far as Jerry knew.

Why didn't Jerry instinctively know his son would predecease him; what had been missing from his own insight that never gave a warning that Jordan was going to die? His chance to help Jordan live his life to the fullest was gone. The doctor gave him a death sentence. He and Jan spent all of Jordan's remaining days trying to find a cure, instead of helping Jordan and themselves to enjoy the last moments.

What was wrong with them that they denied what the doctor said was going to happen. One of them should have known. Even now, Jerry does not get how he missed that fact; that his son, would die.

All the details run like movie trailers round and round inside his head. From morning to night; day in and day out.

A never changing puzzle of what could have been done differently. Jordan had just gone in for a routine doctor's appointment about six weeks before and quietly went through various tests.

Not even letting his parents know until he was sure. Jerry and Jan did not understand why their son had not come to them at once. And why had Jordan not gone to the doctor sooner. Why didn't the doctor know he was sick, sooner? The period in between the time they knew he was sick until he died is packed full of questions. A time that ought to have been used to help Jordan live the life he wanted to live in his remaining days. And losing him killed Jan; literally.

A year later, Jerry knew it was just so flipping amazing their marriage survived. Jan hated him; he knew she did. Then out of nowhere, she got this idea. Before either of them tried to go back to work they would take a nice trip. First for a few months in Mexico and then back through California, stopping at places Jan always wanted to go. They would fly for a change and stay in cozy accommodations, instead of taking the van. The trip of a lifetime Jan said.

Two years had passed since they had left their jobs with most their savings gone for living expenses. And with their savings gone they had begun to use their credit card instead. Before leaving for Mexico they contacted their old employers. Jan was a teacher and was promised a space on the spare list. Jerry could pick up a contract any time he was told.

Feeling hopefully optimistic they took an equity loan out on their condo to pay for the trip. Jerry saying to Jan, "I can't believe they gave us money Jan! We don't even have jobs. No wonder so many people are in debt!"

"Don't be such a kill joy Jerry! Why do you need to spoil

it? I need this trip; we both need this trip. I don't want to talk about money. Please Jerry can we just go please."

Jan had been right of course; they did need the trip. They both felt healed by the heat. Every day Jan made the bus ride into Puerto Vallarta where she sat in a beautiful church and wept. Every day she did this.

They took art classes and cooking classes with locals at a community centre and felt gratified as they used a kind of sign language and gestures back and forth with their instructor. When that did not work, they tried out a bit of butchered Spanish learned over the Internet in the weeks prior to the trip.

Their last stop on their way home was Palm Springs. Jan had always wanted to go there. The weather and relaxed atmosphere of where they stayed had a wonderful effect on the couple.

The day before their flight home Jan said, "Can we stick around here today, swim in the pool, suntan and drink margaritas?" And they did. Laying out on a double lounger. For the first time since the day they were to go zip lining Jerry saw love in Jan's eyes.

"Let's go lay down in our room Jerry?" Stroking his rough cheek with one hand and stroking his chest with the other, Jerry got the message. "OK. That sounds beautiful."

Jerry liked to replay this part best; the part where Jan had two orgasms then they lay and talked. Jerry talked about future trips in the van and Jan talked about something Jerry never wanted to face, "Just in case I die I want you to be happy." She told Jerry. "I want you to get married again." Her hands cradling his head, stroking his shoulder. They made love again then fell into the deepest sleep.

When Jerry woke up Jan was not next to him. The bathroom light was on and he could hear her but did not know what she was doing. He went in to join whatever it was and found Jan on a wet floor. He thought she was struggling to breathe.

An ambulance came within minutes it seemed and they got Jan stabilized right away. A heart attack: a major heart attack and they needed to perform an operation. Jerry remembers asking the doctor, "So what do you say, when you're in a strange country and it turns out your wife needs a surgery?"

He does not remember what the doctor replies and finds it odd that is the way it goes. All the things he says, all his little gems, he remembers word for word. Trying to remember replies, and there is nothing except - a big blank page.

Two weeks later Jan seems to be on the mend; then another heart attack in the night. Jerry had just gone to walk the hospital grounds and catch the sound of the quiet desert pre-dawn. About thirty seconds after he walked out into the hall, she had another massive heart attack. They did not get help for her in time.

Jerry was not there to save her himself either or be with her when she went. Jerry returned from his walk and they had already covered her face with a sheet and were preparing to remove her body from the room.

Jan's body had to be flown back to BC. When Jordan died, they bought two plots at Mt View Cemetery in Vancouver: one for Jordan and one for Jan. She said at the time "I want to be buried in the plot next to Jordan.

You want cremation Jerry, but I am going to be right here next to our son. We will be dead, so it does not matter if we are not together. I know you don't care what happens to you once you're gone but I want to be next to Jordan."

All these messages and gestures put a wedge between

husband and wife. Jerry felt left out. There was no 'them' to the equation anymore. Jan apparently did not even want to spend all of eternity close to Jerry.

She acted as if she owned Jordan. In the hospital that last night she talked of Jordan and all his accomplishments, her maternal worries, her memories. As if Jerry's part in Jordan's life had been inconsequential.

Jan had been chatty about their trip together, telling Jerry she felt ready to go back to work creating some sort of routine. "Jordan wants me to get a life Jerry. I know he does. He does not want to know I have folded up on myself like a poorly built house of cards. He wants me to get back to things."

Jerry sat on the bed stroking the back of her hand. He had no idea what Jordan wanted him to do and Jan had not mentioned there was a message for him. Jerry did not even know where his son was. Jan claimed right from the start that Jordan was right next to her trying to guide her through her grief. Saying he was in a parallel universe.

Just before Jerry went for his habitual predawn walk, Jan told him again that if anything happened to her she would expect him to remarry right away. This time she included Jordan, "Both of us would want you to remarry Jerry; you can't be alone.

"We've had too much happiness for you to be alone. Jordan and I wouldn't want that for you." Annoyed by how the talk had turned to her death, Jerry walked out with no goodbye. All she saw was the back of him as he left.

His only comfort for the next week was the knowledge; she would have thought she was going to see Jordan in the parallel universe she talked so much about. If she was conscious of what was happening, that is. Jerry knew he would not ever see either of them. Not ever again.

It would not be for another year that he felt their presence and when he did, he thought he had lost his mind. He saw them together waving at him through the trees at a favourite picnic spot in Stanley park.

TEN DAYS after Jan's funeral Jerry collected the mail. There were a multitude of cards of condolences, they were meaningless to him. When Jordan died Jan loved people for thinking to send a card. And the cards that had arrived through the mail with handwritten memories of times with Jordan were treasured the most. Jerry had done two things before her coffin closed for the last time.

He removed all her rings; this was an afterthought, when he imagined a grave robber coming in the night, cutting off all her fingers to get at them. He had to ask for help because her hands were clasped together so tightly. The next thing he did was place all the cards and letters she loved so much in life, right next to her body in death.

In Jerry's mind she would have time alone with all those cards of condolence she treasured so much; with all of eternity to mull them over. Hers was a closed casket, by request. She did not want anyone to see her at her worst, except Jerry of course.

Cards from people Jerry did not know, people Jan had worked with, had gone on courses with and from her grieving mothers support group, from her book club, writing group and on and on they came. Cards and letters arrived every single day. Jerry left them unread and unopened in a large mop bucket by the front door.

Then an envelope from the health insurance company came. He did open that one. Inside was a letter that did not even surprise Jerry because he just didn't give a damn any longer. It was a letter denying his claim.

They would not pay the $374,000 in medical expenses owed to the hospital in Palm Springs because they said she had a known pre-existing condition. Jerry sure did not know about a pre-existing condition.

Jan either kept it from him or did not care enough about living to follow up on it herself. Never considering disputing the ruling, the days that followed felt like a relief to Jerry.

A decision had been made for him, freeing him of all the stuff in his condo. All the things that bound him and reminded him of all he had lost. Milling around these rooms was pure pain. His memories should have been those of happy days. His memories though were filled with shared grief of losing Jordan. Jerry could not handle that at all.

Within minutes of reading the letter, Jerry called the strata council president, to ask if they still had a list of purchasers interested in buying in this building. As it happened, they did. Not a surprise he had a fabulous view, with a location right on a nice walkway along the water.

Jerry got rid of all their stuff except, photos, journals, bits, and pieces that had made up their lives including camping equipment and extra bits and pieces for the van. Jordan had little still here except for small gifts given over a lifetime. Jerry kept only one. A small ceramic cat, Jordan made in grade six. It had been Jan's most precious possession and now his most precious reminder of their life together.

Two people totally devoted to the love of their son. When Jordan was little whenever they heard the phrase - the gift of life - he and Jan shared a look. Jordan was their gift of life; a gift for the two of them and a gift for all the people who knew and loved Jordan.

One of Jan's friends from her bereaved mothers support group offered to take charge of selling everything off for a 5% commission and he said, "Knock yourself out!" But when she asked him, "Would you like me to donate the money raised to cancer research or Heart and Stroke?" Jerry's reply was instant and furious, "NO F'ING WAY!" Then he just stormed out of the front door.

Surprisingly, it is not long for all the big and valuable stuff to get sold on an auction site and soon Jerry had a fat cheque from the woman in Jan's support group. He was not in the least bit grateful. By that time, his anger consumed him.

Jerry had it together enough to add a condition of his own in the contract of purchase and sale on his condo which was delivered within twenty-four hours of his call to the strata council member. In the conversation Jerry had with the Strata president he mentioned the price he would accept. Nothing less, but he knew he could have gotten more if he were willing to wait.

The conditions he included were, unconditional use of one covered parking spot for a period of one year. And the unconditional use of one storage locker for a period of one year and unconditional use of the mailbox number attached to his condominium for a period of one year. He said he could be out in thirty days or less. And it was less. Jerry packed up his van and planned a reunion trip across Canada.

He got as far as Hope. He decided to turn around as soon as he saw the sign, Welcome to Hope. "Are you kidding, there ain't no F'ING Hope!" He screamed over and over. Pulling in at exit 65 Jerry was imagining a cup of coffee at the Husky station as soon as he got to the spot it had been for so many years. The restaurant favoured by truckers was closed and completely gone. "Shit."

Another family tradition evaporated. "That does it." Not even driving further up the road and a chance to put in a food order at another restaurant, Jerry turned the van around and headed west and back to Vancouver.

CHAPTER SIX

$\mathbf{M}$avis cannot get used to her new hairdo. It is not the style that throws her, it is the colour. How many times these last few days she has been tempted to go back to Owen for a redo, she can't count. She has been waiting for Monday. Mavis plans to gauge her daughter's reactions and go from there.

Bethany, Mavis's youngest daughter is going to be at Doreen's tonight too. Mavis thinks her latest look deserves a family celebration. She is making every effort to impress with her meal preparation today. Her plan is to get there a bit earlier than usual and give the house a bit more of a cleaning for Bethany's sake.

As untidy as Doreen is, her youngest daughter Bethany, is a total neat freak. The pleasure found in orderliness is one thing she gets from Mavis. Well that and her dark eyebrows. Bethany doesn't like going to Doreen's, "because it's always such a mess," she's told Mavis more than once, "just stepping in the door makes me gag mum." When she does agree to go, it is up to Mavis to get her there with a promise of a meal cooked especially to her liking.

When Mavis called, Bethany's current partner Lynn, answered. Right away Lynn was all, "Oh can I come too?" "Of course, you can dear," is all Mavis says. In the end she is sure Bethany will veto that. Mavis does not want a whole big audience there anyway.

Bethany sounded intrigued and excited when Mavis mentioned a surprise; she asked if she could bring something. Could this uncharacteristic show of generosity be the influence of her new partner Lynn, ponders Mavis?

Cooking a special vegetarian lasagna tonight, is another reason Bethany said yes. She had gone vegetarian two partners ago. Laurel was her then partners name and an extremely sweet girl, so kind to Mavis too. Mavis made a habit of not getting attached to any one partner, but she viewed Laurel, as the one who got away and they stayed connected from time to time.

Laurel as it turned out was only trying on the lesbian lifestyle and now, she had a husband and a baby on the way. Laurel has gone back to eating meat too; it is one of Laurel's vegetarian recipes Mavis has made for tonight. To go with the lasagna, she picked up a bag of the only salad Doreen will eat. A kale mix: it comes complete with packaged dressing. Not the homemade Mavis likes.

As she gets ready to go, she carefully packs an appetizer dish, two bottles of red wine and an apple pie, into her plaid shopping cart. As a bit of an afterthought she pulls out one of her frozen TV dinners popping it on top and a little wax paper package holding a few pieces of chopped up cheese. When she sees them at the bus stop today, she will make sure to give Jerry this small offering for his canine pal.

Slight panic hits when Jerry and Jack are not at the stop to meet her. Walking back along the block very willing to miss the next bus, she finally spots Jerry through the window of the pet store she has seen him going into one other time.

Her heart surges up in her chest; she is so relieved. Opening the door with a confidence she has never felt before, she steps inside. Gert automatically casts a look up when she hears the door buzzer.

There stands a woman with her eyes firmly planted on Jerry's back. But he seems unaware of a new person in the store. Gert silently wonders, who can this be and what is going on? Mavis clears her throat, then speaks so quietly, Jerry does not hear a word, "Isn't Jack with you today?"

Hearing his name Jack rushes out from behind the counter into the store squealing with excitement. Jerry finally looks over his shoulder to see what the commotion is all about. It is the dark eyes he recognizes.

She is early today. If she had not come in the store, he would have missed her completely and need to wait another whole week for his next chance of seeing her again. Briefly he wonders if she is here to look for him and if so, how she would have known where to find him.

Before he can ask, she volunteers, "I didn't see you at the bus stop...so... I thought I'd just pop in here for a minute in case you were picking something up for Jack."

Gert looked from one to the other, "Introductions please Jerry?"

"What? Oh sure," a rattled Jerry wasn't expecting this, "Gert, this lovely lady is my new friend, Maeve. Maeve, this sweetheart here, is my good friend Gert. Gert owns this store and is responsible for getting Jack and I together."

The two women smile at each other and Gert began pointing out treats Jack liked. Jerry marvelled at how Jan could start talking with other women as if they had known each other forever. Reflecting now he thinks this is a universal female trait. Grabbing up the leash, Jerry jingles it to get Jack's attention; he snaps it on.

"Jack needs some fresh air. Care to join us Maeve?" Maeve said, "nice to meet you," waving goodbye to Gert who silently sang a song of joy that Jerry had a new friend. There was hope for him.

Outside they stroll over to the now empty bus shelter. On these beautiful fall days people stand in the sun, soaking up the vitamin D. "How have you been Maeve? It looks like you have been busy; you got your hair cut. You look really nice."

"Oh. Yes, my goodness, I did! I did not even think you'd recognize me. I certainly don't. When I catch my reflection, I mean."

"Oh no Maeve, I'd recognize those unusual black eyes anywhere. And your natural hair colour – this is your natural colour is it not; the lighter colour compliments the darkness of your eyes. It is nice. Oh no let me revise that - the style is genuinely nice on you and if you don't mind me saying so, you were already very nice...to me."

This string of accolades sends a thrill of giggles up and out of Mavis's mouth. "Did you forget my name? It's Mavis, not Maeve."

Jerry feels the smile on his face; its tendrils lighting up his body with warmth making all the dead bits come alive. "For such a sophisticated lady, to me you will always be Maeve. Did you ever wonder what your name means by the way? I can tell you about Maeve, but I am afraid I do not know what Mavis means. Maeve means - intoxicating woman." It's Jerry's turn to be thrilled when he sees how easily he makes Maeve blush a second time.

Now that he recalls, Maeve was a name talked about as a baby name they would choose if Jordan had been a girl so long ago. Jerry is smart enough not to mention this now. Neither have gone into their personal history yet. All they know is how they feel when they see the other. And of course, Jerry knows this little lady is heading off with a dinner all lovingly packed up and ready for her daughter and grandkids.

Usually he hates to hear mention of family and kids, resenting anyone else's good fortune; but not with Maeve. He urges her to share her stories saying he has no family he wants to speak of, now. A need not to muddy new waters with sad stories of his own makes him cautious of sharing. Out of her bag she pulls the little wax paper package and hands it to Jerry for safe keeping.

"You are so good to Jack; I almost feel jealous." And the next thing he sees, is her pulling a dinner out for him too just as her bus pulls up. Ignoring it she says she will get the next one. And as they talk two more buses come and go until Mavis knows if she is going to get there today at all, she needs to say her goodbyes.

Not daring to hug as they both want to do; Jerry takes her arm, guiding her to the bus. As soon as the driver sees the dog he shouts, "No dogs allowed; unless they are in a carrier!" Apologetically, Mavis shrugs her shoulders at Jerry and gets on the bus that will take her to the sky train station.

MAVIS IS out of breath from hurrying the last blocks to Doreen's. Rounding the corner of the town houses she sees with dismay a sour looking Doreen standing on Ricki's doorstep. Doreen spots her mother's familiar tartan shopping cart. The first words out are, "OK, who took my mother?"

A smiling Mavis feels relief. Until this moment she realizes she has been expecting ridicule. Poor Mavis will not have to wait long for that. Ricki's body tenses when out of Doreen's mouth comes a wretched insult. Ricki grabs at Doreen's wrist hissing, "I told you Doreen! Don't you ever talk to Mavis like that."

Turning to Mavis, Ricki smiles weakly and tells her, "Doreen's had a few drinks." As if that will forgive everything and it almost does until Doreen repeats the essence of what she said the first time. "Well Mother? Tell me, what are you all tarted up for? Please tell me this ugly hairdo isn't the f-ing surprise."

Lurching out of Ricki's grip, Doreen stumbles down the few stairs, staggering toward her mother. She yanks the wheeled cart right out of Mavis's shaky grasp. "Oh, and by the way - you're late! Bethany has been here for 45 minutes already. Dinner should be in the oven by the time I get home. You know that - you old cow!"

It is déjà vu. In this cruel comment Mavis hears smatterings of Robin all over again. Shame is what she feels; complete shame for letting her daughter down. Bile rises in her throat. Bethany pokes her head out of the door just then asking, "Hey who are you yelling at out there Doreen! Keep it down!"

Bethany spots the tartan shopping cart but does not recognize her mother at all. She stands like a deer in the headlights "Where's mum Doreen?"

"Right in front of your stupid eyes - you stunned moron."

Bethany's mouth drops open, "Mother! You look gorgeous! Is that why you're late? You have been putting your new-look together? Wow!" Bethany shoots out of the house and out the gate to throw her arms around her mother. To an idle onlooker the hold Bethany has, of Mavis; clutching her small grey head to her bosom, makes the gesture look like a wrestling move.

Bethany swoons, "I love your hair cut. But not the colour Mavis. It's just not you at all!" And that is Bethany. Mavis knows exactly what she can expect from her youngest. Never giving a full complement without snatching it away in a flash of insult. What kind of teacher is she if she cannot even be kind to her old mother?

Stepping away from the embrace while trying to gather back some small part of her pride, Mavis smooths her hair with trembling hands. "Thank you dear." Ricki is still standing on her porch, she calls out to Mavis, "Hey - Mavis. You look smashing and don't let these two tell you different."

Doreen pinches Mavis's arm in a vise like grip propelling her mother the few steps to the townhouse and into her kitchen. Mavis's buoyant mood of earlier today is deflated. She blames herself for getting here late; she should have been on the bus on time. She knows what Doreen is like.

She is just like her father; expecting dinner on the table the minute she walks through the door. With Robin though, she got a physical slap if it were not laid out on the table just so. All she gets from Doreen is verbal thrashing and a harsh pinch if Doreen is out of sorts. Mavis is not sure which is worse.

Putting some hustle in her normally smooth and easy movements, Mavis gets the dinner in the oven to warm up. She opens a bottle of wine, lays out the appetizers and starts to put the dressing on the salad. "What's all this for then Mum," sneers Doreen. Her red rimmed drunken eyes are reminiscent of Robin at his worst. Sitting down at the head of the table Doreen tells her mother and Bethany, "Hubby ain't going to be here tonight.

"First of all, he can't stand the company of a lesbo and second he hates vegetarian cooking. So - Mavis - he has taken some of my hard-earned money and gone out. For a decent meal. Actually, he told me not to tell you but - he hates your cooking anyway and how you look at him like he's a bank robber or something."

Bethany tries to get a word in and is interrupted by the sound of a loud crack as Doreen's daughter, Charlene, hits the wall with the flat palm of her hand. "Knock it off! Why are you so mean to your own mother! I cannot stand it. And you wonder where I get it from. Just shut up!"

"Well, that's a first." Bethany has often wondered why someone doesn't tell her older sister to shut up. "OK ladies, everyone just keep calm. I want to hear your surprise Mum. What is it; come sit down?

"Would you like a glass of wine?" Shaking her head, no at the absurdity of the question, Mavis mutters quietly, so no one can hear, "I don't drink during the week or hardly ever Bethany." Pulling out a chair, she sits, just as she has been told to do.

Her legs and hands are shaking. Doreen seems to be getting worse with her fits of anger. Mavis is second guessing her choice to bring wine. Now Doreen will get drunker and drunker, meaner, and meaner. Holding her quaking hands in her lap under the table, Mavis tells the girls there really was not a surprise other than her new hairdo.

Doreen laughs, Bethany is speechless. "You are kidding? Right? You thought you getting a hair cut would somehow make us happy. Oh Mavis - that's just so sad." Then she starts to laugh hard. Tears roll like bb pellets down her fat cheeks.

"Shut up Doreen!" This is it she has finally had enough.

No more tonight, no more ever. Her granddaughter had inspired her. Charlene had been the one jewel along with Geoffrey with so much promise when she was a little one.

Stan had carried her all around their back yard one afternoon when she was a wee little thing. When Doreen arrived to pick her up, she hated seeing her little girl having fun. She had to ruin it when they were all in ear shot. She shouted at Stan, "Put my kid down you old pervert."

The comment hurt Stan irreparably. He never forgave Doreen and never even saw the little girl again at their house because Doreen would not let Charlene come back. Stan's pride did not allow him to go to Doreen's house either.

Mavis has no idea what is going on here tonight and she is not sticking around to find out. She stands. Doreen jumps up from the table, "Where do you think you're going? Did you know Bethany thought this little surprise was all about money? She called me this afternoon on my cell.

"Bethany says one of Stan the man's policies is coming due. That's not it is it mummy dearest?" Taking hold of her shopping cart Mavis turns her back on Doreen but never makes it to the door.

Doreen is in front of her wrestling the cart handles out of her hand. "Sit down! Now!" Mavis does, knowing from experience with Robin it is just best to put up no defence. Act scared, that is always best. But it was not an act then and it is not an act now. Mavis fears her own daughter.

Charlene appears in the doorway, looking over the scene with disgust. Slipping past the back of her aunt's chair she is about to go out the sliding door. Looking back over her shoulder with the same striking blue eyes, like Doreen's, all made up; outlined in heavy lines of black liner and false eye lashes. Looking just like a young Doreen ready for a fight;

all she says to her mother though is, "Drop dead you ugly old bag." And she is out the door and out the back gate in a flash.

It is just them now. Mavis feels real fear. She does not know what Doreen might do. Long ago Bethany, took her lead from her older sister. Doreen pours herself a large glass of wine draining the bottle. "Bethany Hun, how about opening the other bottle, we might need it."

She changes tactics with her mother, putting on a saccharine voice, "Now tell me Mavis, how is life over in - Kitsilano? I hear you really like your new place. Yes, that's right, Geoffrey told me all about it. Sounds really nice mum... that Stan the man, he took loving care of you, didn't he?"

Mavis hates it when Doreen calls Stan - the man. It sounds so utterly disrespectful. Again, Mavis stands up this time for good she decides. To Doreen she says, "Stan didn't like how you treat me Doreen. He left strict instructions to never give you a penny of his money.

"I can give you my own money of course but I am not giving you a penny of his. Now hand me my purse out of the cart I will write you each a cheque, out of my own money. And after that - I'm leaving here and not ever coming back."

Mavis scribbles them each a cheque for five thousand dollars. She knows the cheques will go through but intends to put a hold on them first thing tomorrow morning. This time she will get an apology from her daughters even if she must buy one.

Still very much afraid, Mavis poises herself to take the next opportunity and try to leave again. Charlene and Ricki sidle into the house; it is obvious to everyone; Charlene went for help. "Come on Mavis. Charlene is looking after my kids while I drive you home."

Mavis has never gotten a ride home from either of her daughters; usually everyone is too drunk. Ricki, a person who Mavis has never warmed to until recently, surprises her again in less than a month, this time with her compassionate generosity.

On the way home, Ricki tells her she likes the new hair style, "It's really nice." But when Mavis mentions updating her wardrobe soon too, Ricki says no. "Your style is classic Mavis, stick with it and before you know you'll have a new man in your life. If that's something you want.

"And if you're lucky he will be every bit as good a man as your Stan sounds like he was." Ricki says it as a joke on Doreen, but it gives Mavis a bit of hope. Without thinking Mavis tells Ricki she has met someone. But as soon as the words are out, she worries Ricki will tell Doreen.

As if reading the worry in her mind Rickie asks, "Is this something you want Doreen to know Mavis?" Mavis is quiet all the rest of the way home. Ricki chatters on about her job, school, her kids, her life. When they get to the house Mavis asks Ricki in, just to be polite. Ricki says, "Oh no thanks I gotta get home to the kids. I need to be up early."

"Well …thank you very much Ricki; for everything. You are a good girl." Mavis means it too. As she's unlocking the back door, she hears the scuttle of footsteps and just as she imagines she has met her maker, Ricki rushes up to stand next to her saying, "Changed my mind. Can I use the loo? It's a long drive back to the bowels of Surrey."

Mavis welcomes her in and while Ricki uses the washroom, Mavis gets out a little bit of cake she has put aside. "Would you have some cake before you go? And tea or water maybe? You probably don't drink coffee so late at night?"

Ricki looks around the kitchen peering into the rest of the big open room shrouded in darkness. Turning on the lights, Mavis gives Ricki a quick tour. "The girls have never been here. Only Geoffrey has...and now you."

Ricki feels so sad for Mavis. Her own mother is not six months in her grave. Ricki misses her every day. Ricki always had a close relationship with her mum. And thanks to her mother, in another couple of months Ricki will be given an inheritance that will take her far away from Doreen.

CHAPTER SEVEN

Ricki watches Doreen slathering on lipstick, in her own back yard, while barking orders at the twins. This is Doreen's way of getting herself ready to bring the youngest two over to be babysat. Ricki does not like Doreen anymore and feels sorry for her kids and for her mother Mavis. Ricki wonders why she is the one looking after the kids when Doreen's old man does not even have a proper job. He could easily do it.

As far as she knows he does something shady. Every time she asks, Doreen gives her standard reply to questions she does not want to talk about, "If I tell you, I'll have to kill you." At first Ricki thought this comment was funny, but now - not so much. Doreen is a user and a liar.

When its Doreen's turn to look after Ricki's kids, Doreen often has an excuse made why she just cannot do it. Ricki ends up looking after Doreen's children again or scrambling to sort out childcare for both their kids. Charlene though, she can be counted on. Ricki is sure; Charlene babysits to get away from her mother.

In September Ricki started attending college at night to

finish two courses for her program; Charlene comes over after dinner to stay with the kids. Ricki gives the kids a bath before she goes. Charlene's job is to make sure they get their homework done and gets them to bed with a story. After that Charlene takes care of her own homework and studies like mad.

Doreen cannot remember what the course is called or what Ricki's job title would be once finished. Ricki told her the last time she asked, "I'm going to be doing intake at the hospital, for when you go to have ex-rays or need lab work - or in the emergency room. It's called triage … I'm doing my practicum next month, so I'll need someone to look after my kids' full time.

"Obviously, I won't be able take your kids next month Doreen; have you got someone else? I hope so. One of my classmate's mums said I can leave mine with her." Doreen's reply had been that Mavis would just come and stay over during that time and not to worry about it.

Ricki wondered if she should mention the baby-sitting arrangements to Doreen again. Mavis would not come after what happened when Bethany was there Monday. Ricki is quite sure of that.

Doreen comes up the steps she has a big smile on her fat face. Ricki feels like wiping it right off, so she baits Doreen with, "Wow Mavis sure has a lovely place. And what a sweetie she is, insisting I come in and have some cake. She showed me around too. You should have told me how nice her place is."

Doreen's face turns bright red; she lacks insight to know Ricki is playing a head game with her. Each time Mavis has invited Doreen or even Bethany to see the new place, they both manage to produce some excuse or other. Ricki acts so self-righteous, Doreen is not about to let on to Ricki that she has not been there even once.

Geoffrey filled Charlene in on all the details anyway and Charlene told Doreen. So, she just lies, "I know right? It's a cute little place isn't it? Perfect for her and she even has a little garden. Did you see it or was it too dark?"

Ricki has her arms folded tight across her chest. Doreen is sensing Ricki is sneering at her for some reason. She looks so smug. If she didn't need Ricki to babysit today, she would mop that smile right off her face and tell her how she and Bethany had squeezed five thousand bucks out of the old bag last night. Chances are, the holier than thou Miss Ricki, would just sneer some more.

Instead Doreen says, "Oh by the way, don't worry about my kids next month; I told Charlene she'll have to stay home a couple of days a week from school to help out. Ricki's arms dropped to her side. Clenching her fingers into white knuckled fists, "You're kidding, right?"

Stunned Ricki says it again, "Doreen! You are kidding, aren't you? She loves school; you cannot make her stay home. You should apologize to your mother. If you do, she will come to stay. Do not make Charlene miss school. Come on ...Doreen?"

Too late Doreen knew she made a fatal flaw. Miss Ricki is all about bettering herself and she wants the same for Charlene. Standing tall, Doreen looks her friend straight in the eye. It's Doreen's turn to sneer this time, "First of all Ricki - my kid - my decision! And - you must be kidding if you think I'm apologizing to that old bat! I'm not.

"Do you think after last night I'd ever have Mavis back here again? Not after how she acted. Not a chance." They both know this last comment is a cover up because it is

Mavis who will not ever happily set foot in Doreen's place any time soon.

Mavis is walking down to Broadway to buy some olives and other supplies from the Greek Deli. As she approaches the store, she hears the familiar rumble of a bus coming up behind her. Instantly hopping onto the Bee Line instead of doing her shopping, Mavis giggles at the unaccustomed spontaneity. Rarely does she veer off her predictable course.

But today is sunny and bright and she has a glimmer of hope that if she heads down the road a little way, she will run into Jerry. Getting off the bus at the stop they first met, she realizes how actually hopeless the prospect seems.

Mavis takes a chance and pops in at the pet store. Gert seemed like a friendly person; and while she is there Mavis will buy some treats for Jackie. When the door opens to the pet shop, she sees Gert.

She stands in the same position behind the counter as if she never moved since last time. And indeed, she had barely moved since she got there first thing in the morning. Gert is pouring over a New York Times cross word magazine and had been at it most of the week.

Holding up the magazine she says, "Jerry got this for me. It's a tough one." For a moment Mavis thinks Gert and Jerry are together, as in, an item. Flashing back to how he opened the door for her on Monday, softly taking her arm to guide her out, she does not think so. Mavis feels confident, he shared a goodbye wave with Gert, as one friend to another.

"Speaking of Jerry have you seen him today?" Mavis asks while casting her eyes in all directions except Gert's. Mavis got silence as a reply and was about to say something else when the door tinkled, and a customer came in.

A young lady in a suit with courier bag over her shoulder, walked right over and gave Gert a big friendly hug. "Hi Mum. How's your day going; I hope I can still take you up on dinner?" Laughing Gert says, "sure as long as it's delivery, I've got nothing made up."

Mavis turns to leave but before she can, Gert says, "Hey hang on a second Maeve, I'd like you to meet my daughter, Claire. Claire this is a friend of Jerry's." A look of interest and speculation fill Claire's face.

"Oh really... How long have you known Jerry?" Mavis feels her face flame; swinging her hand behind her she fumbles for the door handle to let herself out of the small shop. Finally getting the door open she is about to go when Gert pipes up, "Does Jerry have your phone number? Give it to me - I'll get you two love birds sorted out."

Shaking her head with a slight smile on her face, Claire tells Mavis not to mind her mother. "She sees budding romances everywhere. But seriously if you need to contact Jerry, my mother can arrange it." Taking the paper handed her way Mavis writes out her number. As an afterthought, she includes her email address too. "There. Thank you, Gert."

When she was out of ear shot Claire looked at her mum, shaking her head. "That was a bit mean of you mother. She was totally embarrassed." Shrugging her shoulders, Gert smiles and says, "Oh well, you know I like to stir the pot just a bit now and then. Anyway, she barely knows the man.

"I bet she doesn't even know he's homeless. It's quite cute to see them together though; Jerry has been making sure he has clean clothes on and has had a shave on Monday's. That's when she transfers on the bus. That's where they met. She was waiting for the bus..." Gert trailed off and changed the subject while tucking the slip of paper with phone number in the drawer; mentioning she'd most likely see him tomorrow.

JERRY IS ELATED when Gert hands him the contact information for his lady friend. He is not at all sure what he will do with it but is glad to have her email. Gert calls out to him when he heads for the door, "Are you going to have her over to your place for a romantic dinner Jerry," she teases.

She instantly feels bad because Gert knows full well, he is homeless, but she isn't at all sure Jerry knows that she has known all along. Throwing his head back Jerry laughs, "a lady like Maeve might prefer something more refined."

Today he is off to the library downtown. Turning he gives Gert a wave, a peace sign and a thank you for looking after his dog Jack for the day. Jack lays behind the counter, alert but resigned to stay indoors until his master returns. He is well used to the shelter of this store.

JACK HAD BEEN LEFT at the store one rainy day by a person posing as a customer. The young woman had come in with the little reluctant dog. Tugging on his leash the dog didn't seem to want to follow her at all. Gert reached into her goodie bag asking, "Can your dog have a treat, it's organic, hypoallergenic?"

The girl seemed a bit unsure but went ahead and answered, "I think so, but he isn't my dog; he's my parents' dog." Gert asked the girl, "He's a Jack Russell, isn't he? I always liked his type of Jackie. Some have long legs, and some have short. I like the ones with the short bandy legs, like your dog."

As an afterthought Gert asked, "Is there something I can help you with?" By this time, the little dog had smelt the treats Gert was holding and was straining on his leash to get at her.

The girl looks up suddenly as if an idea had just hit and asks if she can use the washroom. "But can you hold onto the dog?" Raising her hand to point, Gert says, "Oh sure to both questions... The washroom is that way - it's kind of tight back there but you'll find it."

Gert opens the little gate surrounding the cash register area behind the counter; and pulls the dog in. Sensing safety, the wee dog with its quivering body and a sigh, stepped into the bed Gert keeps there, turned around a few times then lay down.

So, focused on a task had Gert become she almost missed the sound of the buzzer in the back-storage area. Looking up at the security monitor, she saw the coat of the girl disappear out the door a second before the door slammed shut. No point in going out to see if Gert could catch her. The girl would be long gone, by the time Gert made it around her desk and out to the alley. Nope Gert knew what happened, the dog had been dumped.

Why he got dumped she did not know and did not care. This was not the first time something like this happened, but it was usually a box of kittens. Reaching down toward the dog Gert gave his head a rub and held out another treat. She would find a home for this guy; he is cute.

Not too many days after, Jerry stopped in to ask if Gert needed any help of the handyman sort. She had already seen him washing the windows of the neighbouring store.

Before she could answer though something about Jerry caught the little dog's ear and he desperately wanted out to investigate.

"Let me see if the dog likes you first, then I'll decide. You can tell a lot about a person by how a dog reacts to them." Gert opened the gate, and the dog ran out happily jumping all over Jerry. And man could he jump and jump and jump right into Jerry's arms that were finally ready to catch him on the third jump. "Well he likes you. You must be a dog lover? Do you have a dog?"

"No to both questions. I've never been around dogs but this one is nice. What's his name?" A half smile formed on Gert's lips, "He doesn't have one yet. What would you call him?" Roughing the hair on top of the dogs happily panting head, Jerry said "Jack. Like Jumping Jack." Gert threw her head back and really laughed at that one.

When she had calmed down, she told Jerry the reason she laughed so hard was because his breed is called a Jack Russell Terrier. Pausing for a moment Jerry replied, "OK then I'd call him Jumping Jack Russell." Gert placed her hands on her hips said, "Fine then he's yours to keep and I'll throw in a bag or two of food. But only if you clean up the backroom a bit first and do my windows inside and out."

And that is how Jerry and Jack became partners. And that is how Gert and Jerry became friends. Gert knew from the start there was a deep sadness to the man, and it was only after Jerry and Jack were together for a month or so that Jerry confided how Jack had saved his life. The little dog restored a degree of hope to Jerry's everyday so he could live on with purpose.

He told her a little bit about losing both Jordan and then Jan and at some point in the story, Gert went over and turned the closed sign around on the door and put on a pot for coffee so Jerry could get it all out. It was the beginning of a friendship that they both counted on. One that seemed like it had been there forever.

Jerry came into Gert's shop less than a year before and she could count on him to come every day or so since. She would miss him if he stopped coming around. If something special happened between him and this new friend, Maeve; she would miss him a lot.

THE LIBRARY'S downtown complex appears huge from the outside. From a block away it resembles an ancient Roman Coliseum or so Jerry imagines. Before getting into the library building where all the books are, you enter a covered curving atrium with roof soaring seven stories above. The enclosed plaza is lined with a coffee shop, ATM, a Tea place and by the slice Pizza.

Undercover all-weather seating is available to library patrons or people just passing through to get a peek at the architecture or taking a short cut to the next street. Jerry was not planning to sit down. But a familiar face stopped him in his tracks. It was the young man, Geoff, from the other day and the other library.

Half rising, the young fellow gestures Jerry over pointing to a chair to have a seat, he says, "Hi Pops. Sit here, join me for a minute." What choice did Jerry have, excusing himself he stepped away to buy a coffee that he cannot afford today and sits down. "This is the third library I've seen you at. Are you researching something, or do you just like to read?" Jerry remains thoughtful wondering how to best answer the question.

"The reason I ask is I do research too, mainly as part of

my function as an archivist at the hospital library. The library I work for loans me or rents me out to other libraries if they need systems set up. That's what I am doing here right now.

"Over the next couple of months; the library is running publishing workshops. They had a new program but now they want to try out another. A bit of my help is needed setting it up. Today will be the maiden voyage for some of the facilitators using the program.

"I just stepped out for coffee when I saw you walk in. They need me to go back in and check on their progress in ten or fifteen minutes but that about sums up the capacity I am here in. If everything is running smoothly then I'll do a review.

"If not, then back to work getting the system set up adequately. My other function is... to act as a trusted courier, I guess you could say. Do you know much about computers Pops? It is all right to call you Pops right?"

"Oh, sure call me Pops...I use the library computer several times a week. But to answer your original question the library is something familiar and a place to go on a regular basis. I am between-jobs; some would use the word retired.

"But I prefer to think of this as a new life. Another transitional period that I am adapting to. And I work on my CV, look for opportunities and partly I keep a routine of being somewhere for a specified time, so I don't get out of the habit of attendance, if you know what I mean?

"Call it a routine of attendance - so to speak. I treat the hours spent in the library as work hours – part time hours." Geoff was intrigued by this man but is not sure why.

He had heard that the man he called Pops was rumoured to be homeless or as Geoff liked to say, a constant outdoors man. When he saw him here though, Jerry had clean waves of thick white hair, was wearing neat clothes; even his nails looked clean. He looked handsome, dignified, and respectable.

"So, when you worked, before retirement, what did you do?" Jerry's one-word answer made them both laugh but neither knew why. "Research." They moved on from that subject to another; one close to both their hearts.

From under a newspaper Geoff slips out a book all about the early 1960's VW Van. Shifting his chair around so they were almost side by side, they looked at pictures of their beloved van and read anecdotes owners had written. "There's a van in this book that looks just like yours.

"Under the picture though, the caption says it was taken in the 80's. But that's the thing about the VW, there just are not that many of them around anymore. That's what makes yours and you Pops - so special. It amazes me that I keep bumping into a guy who owns my dream machine."

When Geoff turned the page stopping at a van that did look just like Pop's, Pop got the shock of his life. The photo was of his wife Jan and their son standing next to the van. A short blurb underneath the photo said the photo was courtesy of Mr. Landvik. Taken just before mother and son, Jan, and Jordan Landvik, left the coast of BC on a trip of a lifetime to the Oregon Coast during spring break, just mother and son. It was a twenty-year anniversary of van ownership.

A minute ago, he had just begun to enjoy sitting down having a coffee; browsing through a book with someone he liked. It almost felt normal. Sitting there, with Geoffrey, Jerry was conscious of his feelings and how his mood shifted and changed. This mood was one of complete relaxation.

Since his wife died, Jerry rarely felt relaxed, except with

his new friend Maeve. And now just when it seemed he was finding his way back to normal the photograph sent a shock through his system. He had stopped thinking of them for a minute while he looked at the book with the younger man. But there they were.

Stunned and speechless Jerry lurches to his feet. Gathering up his few belongings from the table top he abruptly leaves behind an equally stunned table companion. Before he is able to get away, Geoff sees wetness misting Jerry's eyes and realizes he has something new to research.

Pop had a story and Geoff wanted to know what it was and would start with the two people named in the photograph. Tucking the book under his arm, Geoff's eyes never left the door his new friend had exited through.

In the library he went straight to the computer he was most familiar with. Complete quiet surrounding him, he turned up two records of obituaries and began to hobble together a story.

Outside on the sidewalk Jerry did not understand his feelings, did not understand why his family turned up today the way they had. The young man had called him – Pop, then seeing the eyes of his son smiling out at him, out of the blue in a photograph taken by him over twenty years ago. Jerry had no memory of giving permission to use a photo, but he must have. He belonged to a VW club for years, but no longer.

People brushing past as he stood stock still, taking up space on the busy downtown sidewalk; someone touches his arm asking if he is OK. Through tear blurred vision he sees the faceless presence of two young men. Later he says they might have had matching black watch caps on.

In the hospital the next morning an RCMP officer takes his statement but he cannot recall much detail. They took his wallet; they took the keys to his van. Jerry vomited when the police officer asked what had been taken. Asking if he had a wallet or money or keys.

His van would be gone. His driver's license had Mrs. Bergen's address. Wiping a hand across his eyes and trying not to cry Jerry asks, "My Van? Please go check on my van?"

CHAPTER EIGHT

Jerry, unable to walk easily he uses a hospital walker to get around on the first day. He has bruising all over his body from the shit kicking, the cop said he had taken. A young woman walking on the street perpendicular to the alley, was talking on her phone and glanced in the lane.

She saw what was happening and started screaming at the top of her lungs right away. There she stood calling for help over and over with people just walking on by until finally another woman called 911.

In her statement, she said there were two Caucasian men. Both wearing black watch caps or toques, they both had on black jackets and blue jeans; black boots and leather gloves completed their outfits. She felt confident they were not much taller than her.

Running at them full force she said she scared them away but by then their victim was unconscious and bleeding profusely. The two muggers had scattered in separate directions. She said she got there too late which was the result of her rescue.

"I need a phone?" Jerry asks the next time a nurse came

in. He sends her out again for a phone book so he can look up Gert's number. She is the only person he can count on. Besides his dog, Gert has been his only friend for a long time; his best friend. The way he has isolated himself after Jan died limited him to claiming a relatively new friend like Maeve as his best friend. Even if he still had her number.

The many friends he shared with Jan began to wilt away when Jordan got sick. After Jordan died it was very much Jan who kept the lines of communication going. Jerry threw out the phone book when he sold the condo. The friends were one reminder of how he had failed his entire family that he did not need any longer.

Gert waited until the end of the day before driving down to the hospital to get Jerry. She has a feeling he will be staying with her for a while. Before she goes to get him, she takes care of clearing out the second bedroom. Puts clean sheets on the bed and roots out an unused toothbrush for him to use. As an afterthought she writes a list of food and buys groceries to stock the place. Gert is not much of a cook, but she is particularly good at reheating handy meals. So that's what she buys.

Gert gives Jack some dog food then takes him for a quick walk around the block. The shop locked up and for the first time in days she gets her car out of the rented monthly covered parking spot she has. On her drive downtown to St. Paul's Hospital her hands are shaking all the way. It was not like Jerry to leave his little pal Jack overnight. She should have called around to hospitals when he did not come back. Oh well, she was here now; wasn't she?

Pausing in the doorway of Jerry's ward, she sees him sitting on the edge of his bed; his head hung to his chest. The bare skin of his back exposed, the hospital gown hanging open. Instinct tells Gert to not say a word.

Moving closer one of the roommates sees the direction she is going and gives his head a sad shake of condolence. Jerry is in pieces. Silent tears run down his cheeks. Jerry is no longer speaking the roommate whispers.

The RCMP officer had come back saying; his garage had been broken into. His van gone and the main house trashed as well. Fortunately, the old lady living there had locked herself in an upstairs room, opened a window and screamed for help.

His van was gone. The vestige of his old life that kept him hanging by a thin thread was gone. A final piece of what had once united his family was ruined and gone too. Taken without warning or consideration.

EXCEPT FOR ONE trip to check on his landlady and his laneway house, Jerry stayed in Gert's upstairs apartment for over a week: without going out at all. He slept sitting up in an easy chair in the living room.

When he was awake, he sat in the same chair just staring into space. His grief was fresh and exposed. Like a scab all red, crusty, and completely visible to the naked eye. Jerry was in a terrible state and Gert was ill equipped to help in any way at all.

While Gert lay in bed usually thinking of sleep, instead now she lay listening to Jerry shuffling back and forth in the middle of the night, pacing, mumbling and weeping. It sounded like he was trying to work something out or at least that's what she told her daughter Claire.

When she spoke to Jerry, he either gave her the silent treatment or muttered angrily that she did not know what she was talking about. Asking every couple of days if he would like her to call his new friend Maeve, he just stared some more. "Was her number in your wallet Jerry?"

No answer, just more tears. Jerry sat and wept. Gert knew the loss of the phone number meant no hope whatsoever to Jerry. The tears, day or night were not over a lost phone number. The tears were the delayed reaction to the death of his son followed by the death of his wife.

Jerry told Gert the full story of his loss one night the year before. It was before Christmas. She asked if he would like to come to her place to celebrate Christmas Eve. Every year Gert had a party, not a celebration of Christmas as such. It was more a celebration of her own incredibly good luck in having such a fine group of friends.

Jerry, in response at first just said, "Oh no thanks Gert. I've got plans." But later, on a night they shared a meal in Gert's apartment he confided that Christmas was just too difficult a time of year for him. He told her since his son was gone, Christmas and all other holidays and events celebrated by families were hard to take.

Being around others who still had family intact was almost unbearable for his wife, Jan, and now was unbearable for him too. It had all poured out that night. First the story of Jan getting the Van as a grad gift, Jordan's conception in the van, their marriage and all the trips they had taken as a family.

The angst Jordan showed about having to go on a family vacation when he was a teenager. He talked about his parents and Jan's parents. He talked about his son being gay and about the day Jordan told them. Or came out as they say.

They were packing up the van for the return trip up the California coast and home. Just him and Jan, they thought

Jordan was out with his new friend, but he came back earlier than expected to tell them something.

Jordan had tried surfing and was surprisingly good. "We were both so pleased because Jordan had finally made a friend. You know what the high school years are like for some kids? Jordan did not seem to fit in anywhere; he was a bit of a loner. But he had a new buddy, and his new buddy was a bit older than him.

We thought that was OK, maybe some of his maturity would rub off on Jordan." Jerry told how Jordan and the friend spent every day together, even at night; they would go down the beach for a run and not come back for hours.

That was the year Jordan had taken up running for the first time. Jordan was clearly happy; happier than his parents had seen him for a long while. Jordan was sixteen, the other boy; he was a man of 22. "It sounds so young now but back then we thought he was way too old for Jordan." And he was using Jordan, Jan would say to her son later.

The trip home to BC had been uncomfortable for all three of them. Jordan had never wanted to go on a trip with Jerry at least, ever again. Jordan and the boy he met in California stayed connected. He lived in Victoria and was in his last year at University there. Jerry and his wife had been hit hard, by Jordan being gay.

"In truth" Jerry said "I was more shook up than Jan; she accepted that he was gay right away. She just never approved of his choice of boyfriend. Not in the beginning and not ever." The hardest part of the story for Gert to hear was of what happened to Jerry's marriage after Jordan died.

And then to hear the rest of it. Jerry was a heart broken lonely man who had once a happy life and then piece by piece the ideal world had begun to fall apart. Jerry said he wanted to honour that old life and the lives of his family, by looking for the good every day.

So, when Jerry introduced Gert to his new lady friend, Gert felt a slight hopefulness for a companionable future for him. Gert could see during the introduction a part of Jerry hidden from her so far. It surfaced and showed itself in a bright and shiny light. Jerry was happy.

Gert could not remember the details of when and how he had met Maeve. She really struggled to recall the whole conversation, but she tended to stop listening when people were talking about what she considered the mundane details of life. She had not exactly paid attention, had she?

To help she asked, "What day of the week did you first meet your friend Maeve, Jerry?" If she knew what day it had been, she could wait at the bus stop Maeve transferred from, to get to Surrey. Gert felt Maeve was the answer to putting Jerry back to rights. But she never asked him what day it was more than once; she just did not have the heart.

JERRY HAS NOT BEEN out of Gert's apartment since the afternoon he got out of the hospital. The little dog Jack, stays down in the shop with Gert during the day, getting out for a walk when Claire stops by later in the afternoon. Claire usually brings dinner for all of them with her when she comes.

Claire wants to contact victim assistance on behalf of Jerry. She is uncomfortable doing so without his permission though. And he does not want her to.

By now Gert had filled Claire in on how Jerry had lost his son to cancer and then a year later, his wife to a massive heart attack in Palm Springs. She told Claire she didn't really know the full details, just that the health insurance would not pay up, so Jerry sold the condo he and his wife owned to pay the bill. "The van was all he had left; pictures of his son and wife were in boxes under the vans bed."

Hearing about losing his wife and son, Claire doubled her efforts with Jerry. Each night when she brought dinner and Jerry was sitting in the chair with Jack on his lap, Claire asked a few questions and then remind him about the victim assistance number. Both Gert and Claire felt helpless.

Especially Claire who was so used to putting things right for people, either by winning their case in court, or giving a family closure. Jerry and his missing van made her feel hopeless; there was little she could do.

What she did do, is have Lynn, her legal assistant put calls in to the police department every day to find out if the van had turned up. And finally, ten days later, she got good news. Two weeks after the van went missing, Lynn decided to call the big towing companies herself, instead of relying on daily reports the police department posted.

She got a few suggestions from the first Vancouver towing company to give a call across the line to Washington State tow yards. During the second call Lynn got inventive and offered a bit of background on the missing van. After hearing a bit of the VW Van's story, the woman on the other end of the phone promised to send out a few emails of enquiry to van clubs, collectors, and parts dealers that she had contact info for.

Lynn gave her the VIN identifier number, license number and as much of a description as she could. Three hours later some results started to filter through. A VW van and young driver had turned up at a garage in Bellingham asking about covered storage. From there the garage owner picked up the phone and distributed the VIN number to figure out correct ownership.

So far it had been there about a week and the police, who were now notified of its existence would be around. The fortunate news was because the van was a collector item it had not been damaged. But the alternate news was not so good. The van had to be held a further few weeks until country of origin and ownership could be firmly proven. And then transport could be arranged.

Gert imagined Jerry ecstatic when he heard the news about his Van but all he said was, "Thanks for letting me know." After that Jerry started going out. Most times the little dog stayed behind; poor little Jack was in a funk too.

Most days he just lay in his basket behind the counter with his head pressed between his front legs. Dull eyes open staring straight ahead. Ears ever alert for the return of his master.

When Jerry did take Jack out, word was from those who saw him; he travelled the back lanes keeping a low profile. Eyes averted, shoulders down, head down too as if in search of something lost. Scanning the ground for an answer not readily found.

The usual happy go lucky Jerry was gone. He stopped offering his services to local businesses for spare change. As far as Gert knew he no longer went to the library and completely stopped volunteering at the food bank. And no longer splitting his bottle booty, as he called it, with the food bank either.

The folks at the soup kitchen called Gert asking where he had gotten to, wondering if he was OK. Not volunteering at the soup kitchen and the food bank was the biggest surprise of all.

Jerry told Gert once, he volunteered there because he

could imagine how easy it would be to become homeless, destitute and without hope. He said he was just one crisis away from homelessness. And that a lot of lonely men were.

DURING HIS FORAYS into the wilds of the Vancouver alley-ways Jerry keeps his eyes open for the two thugs that jumped him. What he sees now but blithely missed before the beating were the number of lost souls just like him. And even as he peers into their faces looking for recognition, now he does not really see them either; he is in his own state of misery.

His clothes are still clean enough to be mistaken for a grumpy old man with a bit of money. "Hey Man, can you spare a loon for a coffee?" He heard the request all day and until his money was gone, he carelessly handed it over. Jerry had not a dime of his own money left.

Gert had said, "Take this Jerry - you earned it and have never collected. I kept track of your hours. Just take it Jerry." And now it was all gone. Gert told Claire later that when Jerry did not turn up for dinner, she noticed he had picked up a few things and left a brief note saying - give the dog to Maeve.

"He already told me to give the dog to Maeve. When I told him I ran into Maeve, remember how he freaked out. He has been on edge ever since mum," said Claire. Mother and daughter both knew Jerry would not be back for a while.

"Martin came around this afternoon to ask about Jerry. He said a pal of his stopped by the other day to show him his new car, a BMW. Jerry came out of the back door just then and you will never believe it, but Martin's pal knew

Jerry from before. He's known him for years; his name is Eric."

"Mum - that's great. Did you get his number maybe he can help out by talking to Jerry?"

"Well that's just the thing; he doesn't want to help out. This Eric guy was Jordan's partner. The one from California. I told you about him – he was Jordan's first love. Martin knows a whole other story Eric cooked up...well in fairness his side of things.

"Now that he knows who Jerry is, Martin has revised what Eric told him. It's complicated but when Jordan got sick his parents wanted to spend all their time with Jordan - which I already knew."

"So why doesn't Eric want to help Jerry? Jerry needs to talk about Jordan and his wife with someone."

"Well that's the other thing. Jordan and Eric lived together for years and bought a place together. After Jordan finished high school the boys moved in together and were together ever since. Martin says Jordan got his degree. I know Jerry paid for it fully; he told me Jordan lived near campus, so he and Jan paid his rent and tuition. Just gave him a monthly allowance."

"Well that's normal isn't it? That's what you did with me."

Holding up her hand for silence so she could continue with her gossip, Gert said, "After graduation and Jordan got an excellent job Eric wanted to buy a condo in the West End. Jan insisted they give Jordan all the money needed for the purchase, so Jerry and Jan sold their house, downsizing to a condo. They had a verbal agreement with Jordan, all their money plus equity, would come back to them if the condo sold or the two men broke up or God forbid Jan had said - you drop dead Jordan....

"And then Jordan got sick and for Eric's convenience Jan spent a great deal of time with Jordan when he was in hospital. Jan must have felt she cursed her son by saying what she said. And it looks like Eric agreed and has not agreed to pay back any of the money given even though Jordan had a huge life insurance policy and survivor benefits through work."

"So how does Martin know Eric? Did you find that out?"

"Of course, I found that out. There is no wrath like that of an ex-lover scorned. Martin and Eric started dating before Jordan was cold in the ground. Eric dumped him for another within a year. And that is what Jan could not forgive and said some things... I didn't hear what but can imagine."

"Did Jerry tell you any of this?"

"Nope. He only said Jordan lived with the bloke he met in California. He never even wanted to mention his name aloud. Just saying by the time Jan died they had lost touch."

CHAPTER NINE

M avis cannot help herself; she keeps looking for Jerry. But after two weeks the penny drops and she suspects he will not call her, or ever seek her out at the bus shelter again. Too embarrassed to stop in at the pet store after the second week of not seeing Jerry she stops coming this way.

No longer seeing Doreen on Monday, she has no reason to come along here anyway. Mavis falls into her own kind of funk. Geoffrey stops by for his usual bowl of soup and can see she is not herself.

When she opens the door, her new hairdo is rolled up tight in pink sponge rollers she used to sport back when her hair was dyed dark brown. She has her house coat on. An old one Geoffrey recognizes as one from long ago days when he stayed overnight as a little kid.

Mavis rarely left her bedroom in the morning without putting on fresh clothes she had gotten ready the night before. When the house coat was new it was saved to be worn after her shower followed by late night TV. But as its aged Geoffrey knows she wears this on days she feels under the weather, as she calls it.

Mavis rarely got sick and would never admit to it if she were. Reaching out to give her a hug she pulls away. "Oh no Gran; do you have the flu? Are you OK? Did you catch something from one of the kids?"

For an instant, some life came back to her eyes, then her shoulders slumped, and she caved into herself again. She tells Geoffrey she has not been to Doreen's and is not going back. "Your mother was so rude to me Geoffrey. When I was there last time and in fact every time I go there, she says such awful things to me. But after the last time, I finally had more than enough. I did not go back, and I will not go back any time soon. Bethany was there too, and they were both - unforgivably rude and unkind. They both insulted me.

"The little boys didn't even come away from their Xbox or whatever it is they have, to say hello, or to say Gran, how are you? If you can believe it? Charlene was dressed like a tart but in her way, she stood up for me."

Rubbing her eyes with the sleeve of her housecoat Geoffrey is shocked again because he knows his Gran is wiping tears from her eyes. Getting her to sit down and spill the beans is not easy; he gets to the bottom of what happened at Doreen's.

"Your sister stuck up for me! With the same kind of language her mother uses. She stood in the doorway and told her own mother to F off! Then she got the neighbour lady. Ricki brought me home; she rescued me from my own daughter."

Gran really gets mad when she tells Geoffrey that in all the time, she has been schlepping dinners over to Doreen it is the first time anyone has driven her home. Ripping her rollers out of her hair one by one, she burst into fresh tears over her hair.

Geoffrey didn't know much but, he did know that no matter what, if a woman made a change to her hair to go easy on any criticism. Last year after having hair to her waist Dixie got her hair cut in a similar style to Gran's. As good fortune would have it, he loved the fresh style, but her sisters did not and told her so.

Geoffrey never heard the end of it for weeks. He had gotten an early education on the do's and don'ts from Doreen. She had a fit if ever she got a bad critique of her many varied hair styles and colours.

Unsure how to go ahead with his Gran right now though, Geoffrey went upstairs got a hairbrush and began to brush his Gran's hair. When he was a kid it was the only luxury, he ever knew of that his Gran allowed herself. She always loved someone, anyone really, to brush her hair and to scratch her back with the hairbrush.

Mavis began to relax with each stroke the bristles made over her scalp. The tension in her body is loosening and almost seeping fluidly out and into the back of the chair. Satisfied that she is unwinding, Geoffrey is a bit stricken by the notion that Stan's been gone two years. Leaning back into the chair she tells Geoffrey; "Stan stopped brushing my hair for no reason given.

"Six months before he died. I should have realized something was wrong. I let him down. If I had seen the signs, I could have made absolutely sure he gave his doctor the right information."

"Gran - Pops was almost eighty. Do you remember last year? You told me when you met Stan; he said how lucky he was to have lived a long life. He was around sixty; about the same age as you are now."

Feeling a wave of guilt Geoffrey says, "I didn't even think about how much you would miss having him brush your hair or having him scratch your back. You can just ask me for back scratches when I'm here you know." Stepping around the chair Geoffrey pulls his grandmothers head to his stomach, allowing them both the comfort of touch.

Her intake of breath shudders in and out as tears of suppressed anger and disappointment fall down her cheeks. Sending her upstairs to get dressed Geoffrey opens the fridge to start some lunch. But when he hears the shower overhead, he thinks, no time being like the present. Pulling out his cell phone he dials his mother Doreen.

"Geoffrey!" Doreen is always surprised, ashamed and completely baffled when her oldest son calls. As soon as and whenever she hears his voice her gut fills with guilt. Though she will never admit it aloud to anyone she knows she has a lot to make up for. She was not prepared for motherhood when he was born.

Explaining it to herself or anyone who would listen she would justify his abandonment as her sowing of wild oats. Too young to have a kid and be tied down by a husband too, she turned to drugs, alcohol, and casual sex for pacification. All this to get her through the motherhood learning curve she would have said if in therapy.

It was the note taped to her pubic hair with duct tape that had forced her to wake up if only momentarily. She had picked up a stranger while stoned. She could not remember who he was or where she found him but the instant, she woke up she knew where she took him, home to her marital bed.

The note said - I have gone to pick up my son and we won't be back. What a laugh, Doreen silently screamed.

Geoffrey was not even Raymond's biological kid. Surely, he must know that!

Hearing something in his voice she can tell by Geoffrey's tone he has found something out he is not too happy about. As poor of a mother as she is, like a little gremlin, she can read how her kids feel. Right now, Geoffrey is speaking in such a hushed tone Doreen turns down her music just to hear. "Geoffrey babe could you speak up?"

Geoffrey hates her calling him "Babe;" she calls everyone babe. All the people she claims to love that is. In his ear it just sounds so false. A failed attempt at painting herself as a loving parent or a kind person. She is many things, but kind is not one of them. Dixie tried to call him Babe once and he almost stopped seeing her; he had such a visceral response.

"Come on Babe - tell Mum what's up?"

"First of all, please stop calling me Babe; I'm not your Babe. Secondly, I am with Gran and she is upset. Do you know why Doreen?"

Flipping things back on Geoffrey Doreen sneers, "First of all do not call me Doreen. I am your mother for heaven's sake." Always so careful with her language around Geoffrey he was one of the few who had not been told to Fuck right off.

"Just spit it out Mother; what have you done to Gran?" Doreen gives Geoffrey a version of a story skewed completely from reality he is sure. Instead of pursuing it, he says, "I was actually phoning to ask Charlene out to lunch on Saturday."

"How should I know what's she's doing Geoffrey? Call her cell and find out for yourself." Doreen never gets asked out by Geoffrey. Nor do the little boys, just Charlene. Doreen feeling angry and jealous that he is wanting to see

Charlene and not her, lets slips that his dear Gran had reneged on a gift she had given both she and Bethany.

"She wrote us each a cheque and then promptly put a stop payment on them first thing in the morning. I have a charge on my account now; I cannot afford a freaking bank charge Geoffrey! Bethany though? Her cheque went through yesterday! That flipping bag favours Bethany because she is a teacher. She had more luck than me Geoffrey I was a mum at such an early age..." Geoffrey stopped listening and opened the fridge again.

He had heard all about his Gran's favouritism all his life. She either favoured him, Bethany, or Stan. Interrupting his mother Geoffrey asks, "Has Bethany spoken with Gran since the argument?" "Well Yeah! She phoned to apologize, the idiot. What did we do? Nothing! We did absolutely nothing wrong. Bethany is a suck up!" If Dixie were here, she would say and had said many times, "Doreen has arrested growth and development."

Doreen has been drinking heavily since she was thirteen or fourteen. The only thing that ever surprises Dixie is Geoffrey and his siblings do not have fetal alcohol syndrome. In fact, the only thing that ever-qualified Geoffrey as having any sort of disability was that he was a genius in certain things. Geoffrey hears the shower shut off. He only has a few minutes.

"I don't care what happened; just apologize to Gran, please? Before you say anything mother, ask yourself, what is in it for me? Bethany apologized she got her cheque... apologize Doreen. Gran is just finishing her shower; pull it together. Now's your chance to try out sucking up for a change. Phone back in ten and say sorry."

Ending the phone call before she could argue Geoffrey pulls a jar of soup out of the freezer then puts it in the microwave on defrost. He cuts up some cheese and tomato and puts some crackers on a plate. There is nothing else. Gran's fridge is almost empty.

Ten minutes later Mavis's phone rings; after a short chat Mavis hangs up. "You called her when I was upstairs didn't you?" Geoffrey does not answer because he knows it is a rhetorical question. Next thing Mavis calls her bank manager that she has been dealing with for years. She leaves a voice message saying to let the cheque go through and if there is a concern about doing so to call Mavis back. That done she goes up behind Geoffrey and gives him a little hug around his waist. "I honestly don't know how you got to be so nice."

Geoffrey just smiles because he knows how; it is Stan and Gran and care and the love they showed each other and the love they lavished on him. "Why don't you ever want money? Stan and I always had enough but you never would take anything. Except do you remember how Stan always bought you a good winter coat each fall and all your shoes?"

Lunch ready, Geoffrey elaborately pulls out a chair for Mavis, lays a napkin on her lap and they both say a word of thanks to Mother Nature before they eat. "After lunch I'm taking you shopping Gran; you have hardly any food in the fridge. But before we go can you tell me what else is going on?

"You've had fights with Doreen before - but I just get the feeling something else is bothering you." Mavis shook her head, no; there is nothing, but Geoffrey sees a telltale mistiness in her eyes before he drops the subject.

Two hours later and a good shopping done they walk out of the grocery store near where Mavis lives. At first, she does not recognize the man propped up against the wall as they pass. He has a hat sitting on the ground with a note attached. Mavis automatically reaches in her coat pocket and slips a fiver in his hat. As she stands to go, she suddenly knows who the man is. Glancing back over his shoulder to see where his Gran had gotten to, he sees her characteristically place the money in the old man's hat.

Smiling inwardly Geoffrey feels pride in her for this natural generosity. Then does a double take of the man. It is the guy from the library, Pops.

His face holds tight to the end days of bad bruising like he has taken a beating. His Gran hurries past him and in a rush says, "Can we go home. It's so cold out." Geoffrey takes another look back at the man on the ground, but his head is turned the other way his hand fondling the fiver his grandmother left behind.

When Geoffrey pulls out of the underground parking the man is gone. He notices his grandmother looking too. "Did you see that man Geoffrey? He looked like he had been beaten up; his whole face was bruised." There is a quiver in his grandmother's voice. She sounds near tears, so Geoffrey decides he will stay the afternoon with her.

They will play scrabble or cribbage, and she can finally show him how to make soup stock. That ought to cheer her up. When he parks, carries in her bags, and gets her making some coffee for them both he calls the library, claiming a family emergency. Next, he calls Dixie and asks her to come here for dinner, at his grandmother's tonight.

Mavis and her grandson never do get around to the games, but they do make soup stock. While the stock is ruminating in the slow cooker the two make themselves comfortable in the living room. Both intending to have a nice chat with Mavis reclining all the way back in her chair and Geoffrey stretched out on the lounge. They both fall fast asleep within minutes.

Sleeping the afternoon away put them behind schedule. Neither wake up refreshed. In fact, they are both more tired after their unexpected nap than ever. At Geoffrey's suggestion, Mavis hustles upstairs to give her hair a comb and apply a dash of lipstick before Dixie's arrival. As an afterthought she runs her new hot iron through her hair, straightening all the curls from earlier in the day. She puts on a fresh grey wool pencil skirt with three kick pleats in the back and a pair of bright tights and a matching cardigan in feeble attempt to cheer herself up.

DIXIE ARRIVES RIGHT on time and with her she brings her younger sister, Bonnie, in tow. Dixie is always of the mind, the more the merrier. Tonight, though as soon as they walk in, she sees Geoffrey has another plan in mind. Mavis looks unbelievable with her new hairstyle but there is deep sadness settling over her.

It is the presence of Bonnie who saves the day when she dramatically shouts out, "Mavis! You look fabulous darling. I positively love your hair and your skirt is out of this world. Who dresses you anyway?"

Bonnie suits her name, always full of enthusiasm. Over statement is her trademark. Mavis gets a bit of colour in her face when Bonnie marches over for a hug.

"Can I touch it? Ewe - it feels like a cat, nice Mavis. When did you decide to do this? Is there a man? Come with me my dear; I brought some wine for the two of us to share. Come to the couch and tell Bonnie all about it."

Leading the way Bonnie goes to sit on the living room sectional lying out comfortably on the lounge end. Mavis sits in her white leather recliner. As usual she is not comfortable reclining in front of guests. Bonnie hops up to get their wine, comes back and begins pressing the chairs controls sending Mavis's chair smoothly back.

"Now – you get comfortable and tell Bonnie all about him. Enquiring minds want to know." Geoffrey and Dixie stay in the kitchen area and begin to lay out a dinner. Dixie has brought most of it. "Bringing Bonnie too – well it turns out to be genius Dix. Thanks!" Whispering Geoffrey fills Dixie in on some of what has happened today.

Cautiously mentioning his mother Doreen's part in it all; knowing Dixie is like his Gran and never judges, makes talk of Doreen easy. Dixie has empathy for Doreen saying this time, "We don't find ourselves in dark alleys without a bit of a push. Who knows what happened to your mother Geoffrey?

"If she would have some counselling, she might make some discoveries. Go easy on her." Later that night he tells her about seeing the guy from the library outside the store, panhandling. And of how touched he was to see his grandmother reach down to give the guy five bucks. And then about her stricken look as she notices the bruising on the complete strangers' face.

Mavis feels restless exhaustion. She cannot sleep. Seeing Jerry again was a shock. He did not even seem to know who she was. Tomorrow she vows to go back to the pet store and find out what happened. But in the morning, she remembers she had given out her phone number and either it was given to Jerry or Gert still has it. Neither of them has called her. She is not sure what to do.

For the first time since leaving her phone number at the pet store and not getting a call, she knows she is edging into the blues. If she goes to the store and is told he just is not interested, or Gert says something indicative of her not realizing they knew each other well enough... Tomorrow - she promises herself. Today though she is going back to the grocery store and see if he is there again.

There is no sign of Jerry at all, but she does see Geoffrey drive by twice. Momentarily she wonders if he was looking for her when she sees the nose of her old SUV edging out for one more pass, she hustles inside the store.

"Maeve? .... Maeve? Is that you?" She spins around when she feels a hand on her shoulder. Standing right in front of her looking genuinely pleased to see her is a young woman she met a couple of weeks before. But she cannot remember her name. Claire reminds her of who she is and asks if she has seen or heard from Jerry.

"Well no I haven't...not since... I dropped my number off...The day I met you. Remember? I wrote my number and email out for your mother to give to Jerry. Do you know if she gave it to him?"

This is so much more forward than Mavis normally is, but she just wants to know. Running into Claire at this moment at least, seems kismet. Claire at once notices the catch in Mavis's voice when she says she has not heard from Jerry. The lady's eyes have misted over too.

Claire who regarded her mother Gert as Jerry's personal information keeper, suggests Mavis, ask Gert about it. Claire honestly does not know what happened to the number.

Looking around anxiously, Mavis promises to stop in at the pet store the next day.

Then as an afterthought she tells Claire about the homeless man sitting outside the store the day before. "I wasn't sure, but he looked like Jerry...Right outside here in front of the store. He was panhandling and I did not even recognize him at first Claire. He looked terrible, like someone had hit him."

Claire is thoughtful for a minute still not wanting to tell Jerry's friend the whole story. Taking Maeve by the hand she says again, "Go see my mum or give her a call. And who knows Jerry might be there too."

But the next day came and went and the illness Geoffrey thought his grandmother had been struck down with the day before was hitting her hard. With a fever and the chills Mavis spent an uncharacteristic day in bed. It will be several days before Mavis is well enough to talk to Gert.

Geoffrey and Dixie take turns stopping in on Mavis. Bringing her store-bought soup; they stay with her to make sure she eats it. Dixie feels sure there is something deeper than flu troubling Mavis. When she gets home on the second day it is Bonnie who tells her older sister what Mavis confided to her.

Mavis told Bonnie that she thought she had a boyfriend. But Bonnie said Mavis also thought that he had dumped her. That was the last thing either she or Geoffrey imagined happening.

The idea of her having a boyfriend is a completely startling fact for Geoffrey. For him, Stan was her one and only. But it seems the new romance has not lasted long and is over before it really got started. Geoffrey feels relieved.

CHAPTER TEN

Mavis is feeling a whole lot better; the sun is finally out after a succession of wet and windy days. And with it the sun brings a new resolve for Mavis. She will try having a shower first and then if she feels restored enough, she will stop off at the pet shop to see Gert. It has been four or five days since she last saw Gert's daughter Claire.

Mavis tries on a new pair of jeans she bought a couple of weeks ago. They are the first jeans she has ever owned in her life and she is a bit self-conscious. They were a perfect fit the salesgirl assured her. But to Mavis they feel tight and foreign. When she puts on a ski jacket, she has had for years but never worn, she does not recognize herself. Gert will not either.

In a way this disguise gives her courage. She feels ever so slightly invisible. And invincible too. She will take the Bee Line at about 2: PM. She is sure Jerry will be nowhere in sight, with his hand out, at that time of day. But from the bus window she spots him sitting on the ground again; this time he is outside a beer and wine store with the hat tipped up hopefully by his side. Mavis pulls the buzzer but when she hurries back down the block he is gone.

Getting back on the next bus Mavis names the feeling deep in the pit of her stomach as fear. Gert is just putting a 'back in fifteen minutes' sign on her door when Mavis appears. Seeing who stands on the other side of the glass Gert ushers Jerry's friend in. "You sure took your time!" Gert snaps. "Claire saw you almost a week ago; why did you wait so long to turn up?"

When Mavis starts to answer the little dog behind the counter hears her voice and starts to whine. He is jumping up and down as if attached to a spring. He tries desperately to escape over the little gate that holds him safe.

Gert hurries over to reach around, lifts the latch and out springs Jack right into the arms of Mavis. Again, so excited to see her; giving her face a good wash. Gert stands shaking her head with a mixture of joy and sadness.

She is not too happy about what she is about to do but she has her instructions. "Look Maeve when Claire told Jerry you would be coming here to see him, he freaked out. We have not seen him since. Pick up that dog again and come upstairs; we need to talk about a few things."

When they got upstairs Gert made coffee and they sat at a dining table covered in books and magazines. It had a perfect view of the other side of Broadway and through the buildings were glimpses of downtown and the mountains beyond. Mavis imagines it must be nice at night sitting at the table with a glass of wine, seeing everything lit up. Jack sitting next to the chair clearly wants to sit on her lap, so Mavis bends down to give him a lift.

Gert stands watching from the kitchen doorway while Jack gives Mavis's face a lick then sits looking into Mavis's eyes as if he has discovered the meaning of life. "Look I may as well get straight to it; Jerry got beaten up. He is not himself at all and none of us knows what happened, but it was right after you left your number with me.

"The last I saw of him that day he told me he was off to the downtown library and that's all I really know. I thought he would email you from the library ... And then when he didn't come back for Jack? Well Jack had to stay overnight here. Next morning no sign of Jerry...and I confess I was feeling a bit ticked off.

"I wait and he doesn't come back at all. No sign of him. No one had seen him. Thank god Jack was here with me; thank god because Jerry got so badly hurt, he had to stay in hospital for a few days."

The look on Mavis's face tells Gert all she needs to know; this lady is more than a little upset. "Who did it; how did it happen? Did he say?"

"A witness said it was two guys... she saw him in the lane getting the living daylights kicked out of him. She called out for help and those two thugs made a run for it. The police and ambulance had to be called. By the time they got him to hospital they figured out his wallet had been taken and his keys. They stole his van Maeve.

"His whole life was in that van. It's found now but I do not think Jerry can afford to pay the various fees to get it back or maybe he doesn't want it back. I think he has had a breakdown of faith.

"Anyway, Maeve when he heard you were coming, he asked me to give you Jack; he took what he needed, then he left. He said you need Jack. So, he is yours. Period."

Mavis quietly listens. She is not surprised to hear what she hears. She tells Gert what she knows too; where she saw

Jerry panhandling and most recently where she saw him today. Telling how she got off the bus after seeing Jerry, but he was gone by the time she got back to where he had been sitting. She tells Gert how she feels about Jerry.

Shyly looking down into the brown beady eyes of Jack who is now her dog she says, "I love Jerry; he's my soul mate. I knew it the moment I saw him. And Jack? Well I love them both, as a package."

Mavis tells Gert about how she is sure the little dog Jack, once lived on her street with a Chinese family. When Gert hears the story, she confirms Mavis's belief. And shares her own tale of how the dog arrived at her store.

Before Mavis and Jack leave, Mavis happily stocks up on pet supplies. She feels somehow optimistic that she will see Jerry again. Having Jack with her would ensure that. Jack brought them all together once and he will do it again. She picks out some new fancy dog dishes, a bag of food, a dog bed, and a small soft kennel that Jack can ride the bus in.

Today though they would do something Mavis has never done before in her life and get a cab home with so much to carry. Jack runs in and out between the two woman's legs and occasionally, gives a sharp bark, as if to say, 'Hurry up!' Writing down her contact information again she gives Gert strict instructions to call any time of the day or night if she hears from Jerry. All set to head home Mavis holds Jack by the leash knowing bringing him to her place is just the beginning of a life change for her.

Getting home and into her little cottage with her new dog feels right. The first thing she does is mix Jack up a bit of dinner and then give him a bath in her tub. He sits perfectly still even under the hand spray. Once out he sits still again on top of a towel laid down for just that purpose on the kitchen table. He stands in clear ecstasy feeling the gentle heat while she blows him dry.

Telling him to stay where he is, she reaches into the bag of doggy supplies removing his new brush and comb. Turning back to him Mavis smiles down to see he has stretched out full length on the towel and is looking up at her, with tail wagging. Exposing his teeth in a grin.

This becomes the morning routine after their first walk. Not the bath part but dipping his feet in a dish of warm water to get the mud off; followed by a good rub down with a towel. If he is very wet, he is lifted onto the kitchen table where Mavis gives him a bit of a blow dry.

It is raining hard when they go out this time. Mavis tries to get him to walk with the new coat she bought but once she gets it on, he stands as still as a statue and will not take a step. Off comes the coat and on comes more rain; he is soaked when they return after a brief stretch of their legs. And just in time for the sun to break through.

Taking the comb to his coat Mavis tries to get as much loose hair off him as possible. "You have too much hair Jack. How on earth can I ever catch up to it all?" Jack lets out a sharp succession of barks, skidding off the table. He sails through the air and lands right in front of the door where Dixie stands looking in through the window.

Swinging the door open, Dixie asks, "Well who do we have here Mavis?" Mavis gives such a vague answer about finding the dog and that he lived down the street but the family who owned him...well they did not want him anymore. Dixie stopped listening to the convoluted sounding story by the time she got to the part about Jerry.

But Mavis stops herself in time from gushing on, telling Geoffrey's girlfriend everything. Dixie tunes in again in time to hear, "It was really this little dog that brought us together.

"He's been looking after Jack for a while you see...And oh he is such a good person he volunteers at the food bank and the soup kitchen and is mostly retired; well at least I think he took early retirement, " Mavis rattles on, "but for exercise he collects bottles and gives half the bottle money to a food bank!" Dixie is nodding her head speculatively recalling Bonnie said there was a broken off love affair. Well it appears that it might be an on again love affair.

"He sounds really nice Mavis; does he have a name?" Mavis is bright red; she abruptly turns to pick up Jack saying simply, "Jerry. It's Jerry. He wants me to look after Jack because I'm not as busy as he is. I have more time to devote to this little guy. Isn't he cute Dixie?"

And seeing him held in Mavis's arms, his white, very rough looking coat with black smudge around one eye; he does look cute. Seeing Mavis stroking his head Dixie cannot help feeling she is seeing a side of Mavis not shown to anyone else; yet.

Dixie has a feeling she will be seeing a lot of Jack. "Can I hold him Mavis?" Jack refuses to be passed over though preferring the arms of his familiar friend. "He might be feeling insecure Dixie; sorry about that.

"Give him a few days and I am sure he'll hop right into your arms. Here! I know! Give him a bit of a treat. He'll love you for it." Holding out the treat for Jack he just stared at it. He made no move toward the treat. Mavis is embarrassed. Jack might have hurt Dixie's feelings. "I'm so sorry Dixie!"

Dixie chuckles, "Oh don't worry Mavis. He probably senses I'm not the maternal type." This comes as a surprise to Mavis. She wonders if Geoffrey would agree and asks if Dixie and Geoffrey might have children someday.

"It's not something we've talked about per se. But you must know Mavis; it is usually the woman who wants to fill the nest? "And I don't want kids. Not yet. I'm not saying no to kids ever Mavis. I have known lots of women, who after years of saying no, will suddenly hear their biological clock ticking like a time bomb. But I don't think that'll be me."

Mavis has no idea how Geoffrey feels these days. But there was a time when he confided in her about everything. The only time he mentioned wanting kids though was with his first real girlfriend. Young and idealistic, when describing her he said, "She is the one Gran! I can see us having kids together."

He might have matured a bit since, but then again; not. "You know Dixie no matter how much trouble Doreen gave me or still gives me without having her; there would be no Geoffrey."

Dixie loves the connection between her partner and his grandmother. The reality is she does not know how long her relationship with Geoffrey will last. Slowly their lives are taking on different shapes. Geoffrey may not need her much longer. And she may not need him.

Jack's getting restless after his shortened morning walk in the pouring rain, so Mavis suggests Dixie join them for another walk. "Oh no I can't Mavis, sorry I have a client in an hour. I need to get ready for that. I was close by so thought I would stop in for a minute. You two can come down to the bus with me though if you want."

Together they all walked out into the back lane and head the short distance to Broadway where Dixie would catch a bus. When they get to the bus stop, Mavis peeks at her watch checking how long the bus will be.

Handing Dixie, the end of Jack's lead Mavis says she will dash into the Greek Deli before it's time for Dixie to go. Jack strains on the leash to see where Mavis has gone. His attention is suddenly caught by a man waiting for the bus.

Straining in the new direction Jack begins to whine and wiggle his body about. The man he sees is Jerry. The bus is just drawing to a stop. Jerry has a choice, and he makes it. Rushing over he gives the little dog a quick pat along his wiggling back. Then on impulse he pulls a treat out of his pocket and tosses it in the air for Jack to catch before stepping onto the bus.

Mavis comes out just in time to catch sight of Jerry's back while he is showing his transit pass to the driver. Standing speechless, Mavis watches him in profile making his way down the aisle as the bus pulls away from the curb.

Dixie noticing Mavis watching the man on the bus she asks, "Do you know him; he just petted Jack. Jack sure seemed to be comfortable enough with him to take a treat. Do you know him? Mavis?" Snapping out of her trance she says, "Oh sorry Dixie, no I'm not entirely sure. But I've made you miss the bus!"

As is the case another bus did come along and on it, Dixie got. But before it arrives, she instructs Mavis to stay connected. Reaching deep in her pocket for the business card she keeps there; she feels cloth; no card.

"Oh well Mavis. I was going to give you my card so you can call my cell any time. But here let me write it down for you." Mavis stares at the slip of paper with Dixie's cell number. Her eyes glassed over; why hadn't she run up to the bus and grabbed Jerry by the coat.

Why didn't she tell Dixie the truth and say she did know him? Mavis was about to confess to Dixie about the little lie she had told when she hears the familiar sound of the bus.

Waving goodbye each woman has a head full of her own thoughts. Dixie suspects there was something Mavis wanted to say but Dixie's appointment cannot wait. Mavis is crest fallen to have let another chance to speak to Jerry slip away.

And ashamed she had not said - Yes, Dixie I do know him. He is my soul mate; the man I told Bonnie about. Excuse me Dixie; I have to go to him - She knew what had stopped her, embarrassment, and pride. Two of the ugliest characteristics a human being could have as far as she was concerned. Mavis owned both. Big time.

CHAPTER ELEVEN

Mavis is up to speed on the rhythm of how Jerry, trained Jack to walk on the leash. The dog does not pull and always seems to enjoy walking close by her side. Dixie is clearly impressed when Mavis tells of how Jack had been a bit of a leash puller with everyone until Jerry came along. "Well how did he do it?" Trying to make conversation Dixie had kept the conversation about the dog going all the way to the bus stop.

Dixie has years of experience with shy people like Mavis. Her intrinsic skill of discovering a person's passion through asking questions is painless. Raised in her large and talkative family Dixie is not comfortable with silences. Her family are loud talkers and nosy listeners. Especially when she was growing up, everyone talked at once. Early on she discovered she could make herself much more likeable by drawing someone else out. Instead of holding court and doing all the talking she tends to ask questions.

The first night they met, Geoffrey said he could not remember meeting anyone else who could talk as much as she did. Since then Dixie's fine-tuned the skill of listening which is the key in her work. Mavis chats on telling Dixie how she found a video online that instructed a dog handler to just stand still when the dog pulls on the leash.

"And then whenever Jack relaxes, he looks back at me and we get on the move again. Until he pulls; then I stop. I never jerk the leash; I just relax and stand still. He knew with Jerry and he knows with me now too when he stops pulling off, we go.

Pulling equals going nowhere. Walking on a loose leash equals going for a nice walk." Dixie looks up with relief realizing all the dog talk shortened the walk and they are at Broadway already.

BESIDE THE LANE are garbage bins belonging to the corner Fast-food restaurant, a man stands motionless when he sees the small familiar shape of his dog. The dog and lady sent a jolt of emotion through him like an electric shock. It has been over three weeks since Jerry got mugged. And a bit longer since he last shared time with this sprightly looking gal; seeing her walking Jack has the effect of snapping him to attention.

The last time he thought of her, he was remembering how she was changing his life. Giving him a sense of hope; a twinkling spot of sunshine on an incomplete life; the promise of the soft rub of a soothing salve called love. Massaged right inside the empty spot he would always have inside his heart. That was the day he was about to go into the library. His plan had been to send her a romantic email.

He had it all sketched out in his mind; he would include an invitation for a picnic lunch at Stanley Park's Third Beach. He was going to suggest any day; rain or shine because they would have the comfort of the Van for all kinds of weather.

On his way into the atrium this had been on his mind. He felt hopeful. With his hasty retreat from the young man and his VW van book; when he got mugged all that hope was soon replaced with despair. It was the day that marked the end of what he had begun to think of as a good existence.

He had seen the glimmer of the light of hope at the end of his very dark tunnel when he met the little lady. He had an ideal place to stay and a few odd jobs that would see him through to retirement. His CPP was about to be applied for, though he had been holding off on that.

Gert reminded him, not for the first time, to check on his qualification for a government survivor's pension. Gert felt sure he would get one from Jan's job too. He had resources. Before the mugging he was readying himself to finally make use of those resources and drag himself back to the world of the living, a world of societal norm. Maybe get a small apartment with underground parking.

Jan would be in shock that his holiday in the van after her death had turned into a way of life. She had been the caretaker of the money but after Jordan's death, her ability to think clearly was clouded even more than Jerry's. They both had resources they could have tapped into.

Spotting his dog walking with the two women Jerry's painfully aware of how low he has sunk in just three weeks. The thugs robbed him of more than his van; they took his hope and dignity. When he went back to see Mrs. Bergen the final blow was struck. His sense of reliability and reputation were now demolished too.

Mrs. Bergen was glad to see him after hearing from the police about the mugging. But when he asked about getting a new key for the garage she said, "No Jerry; sorry I just can't take the chance of someone coming back. My niece says - it's too dangerous to have you live here anymore. I'm selling; but please come in and have some soup.

"You must be hungry with nowhere to stay now." This last remark by Mrs. Bergen laid all the cards on the table. He thought he was flying under the radar of detection, but she knew all along he was homeless. Total mortification swallowed up the rest of his pride.

JERRY PASSED, on joining her for soup. He went back to Gert's but stayed only a little while longer. He could not say where he lived now. For the first time, looking down at the soiled clothing he wore from head to foot Jerry felt shame and humiliation. The door of the restaurant opened and the young girl from earlier peeked out. In outstretched hand she held part of a burger for the man. Nodding a look of thanks her way Jerry shoved the burger in his coat pocket.

On second thought he removed the coat reversing it to the cleaner side. Hustling across the street he gets closer to watch the lady and dog some more. He steps around the corner in time to see a business card drift out of the younger woman's pocket and watch as she takes the dog leash from Maeve. His little dog Jack becomes anxious as he watches his new owner walk through the store entrance.

Straining on the leash Jack pulls toward the door as hard as he can. Jerry wants to go over, pick him up and feel him close but takes an opportunity to bend down and pick up the business card instead.

Jack must catch a familiar scent of Jerry when he does, because suddenly Jack shifts his full attention on the man who seems to be waiting for the bus. Jerry glances over his shoulder to see his ride is there. Hesitating only a fraction of a second, he steps forward and reaches a hand down to pat the dog.

The woman holding the dog's leash, visibly tries to restrain him as he jerks and pulls, trying for all he was worth to get at the man. And when the man leans down the little dogs' sashays back and forth like a snake, wagging his whole body in joy. To the hiss of air brakes, the man stands tall, backs up a few steps and turns just as he sees a familiar head making her way back out of the store.

On the bus Jerry automatically finds a seat at the very back and slumps up against the side of the bus. Watching buildings and doorways go by from his window everything is seen like a movie reel. Moving along from stop to stop all along Broadway Jerry is seeing with new eyes this after-noon the path he has chosen to take. Two hours before he had sat out front of a Beer and Wine store his hat sitting forth as a hopeful vessel; an invitation to strangers' generosity. Fooling himself into thinking living in his van was cool and resourceful; a way to keep him on memory lane.

Now he sees it was just him coasting along on a ride of denial one step away from homelessness. And he is home-less without his VW van that holds so many memories. The rest of his dignity too is lost. So much was robbed right out from under him as he lay beaten and unconscious in a back alley; just like any other old rubbie.

Roaming the lane ways, he runs into others who are headed along the same direction, or already in the same sinking boat of despair. And more still, who no longer bother with scouring through the cast-off stuff for a jewel that can save their day. Using the lanes as crash pads; rolling their bodies in cardboard to stay warm for an hour or a whole night if they are lucky...

People with no hope. Some still with a bit of pride in their ability to stay one step ahead of the end and willing to give aid to a brother. And still others resorting to attitudes of each man for himself - survival of the fittest...

Last night Jerry was rousted from the sleeping nook he had found three nights before. One lone man muscling him out and without too much of a fight Jerry gave up his safe shelter. He spent the rest of the night in a fruitless effort hoping to find dry accommodation. Finding somewhere to be protected from wind and cold was a challenge and a commodity.

Last night he went hat in hand to the soup kitchen he had volunteered at for the past two years. They did not even recognize him. He had become just another face he supposed, or his grizzled beard was enough of a disguise. Keeping his eyes down and his hat pulled low he looked like any anonymous soul. When he left the building, it was not comfort of a hot meal he felt, it was shame. Jerry was slowly waking from a comma.

Gert was right. He was having a delayed nervous break-down. It was time he talked to someone about all he had lost. Flicking the business card, he had found earlier back and forth between his fingers, it flicked right out of his hand into the aisle of the bus.

Not being bothered to bend down and pick it up he continued to stare out the window as the world passed him by. Cautiously, a girl nearby picked the card up off the floor. Silently she thrust it in front of the dirty man's face but not before noting the card said in part, 'Clinical Psychologist.'

Jerry was in a trance staring into his past; he felt the nudge of the edge of the girl's wrist, making a second attempt at returning the card. This time she pointed out the words and said, "You might need this, you dropped it."

For the first time Jerry looks at the words on the card. Scooping it up at the bus stop he hastily shoved it in his pocket. It got taken out of his pocket to unconsciously fiddle with on his ride. "Everything happens for a reason." These are Jan's words and her voice he hears inside his head, speaking as clear as a bell, startling him back to reality.

He grasps hold of the card as if it were a lifeline and looks up at the girl. He promises her that he will pull it together. Stepping back from the seated man the girl fells sure she saved a soul for the day.

Jerry disembarks the bus by the pet store. The sign is flipped up saying, back in fifteen minutes. He slips into the lane to wait in quiet anonymity. The neighbouring merchant's back door swings open. Out steps the business owner Martin, and he sees Jerry standing right in front of him.

Lighting up a smoke he says, "Hey, Jerry glad I caught you. Gert has something for you - if you can remember the combination you can get it now. It's inside with the garbage bins."

Two years before Gert had installed a security shelter for the building's garbage and recycling bins. It was virtually impossible to get into them without a combination. Each of the building's residents had the code. Jerry does not know the code for the bin, but Martin did.

Inside next to recycling was a bike with a basket holding a helmet and, on either side, hung two panniers. It was secured with a titanium lock. He recognized the lock right away. He gave it to Claire when she bought a bike back in the summer when she had an idea to ride to the courthouse.

She rode it once and was scared out of her mind. Jerry

said to just hang onto the lock and told her to keep the bike just in case. "You never know Claire, one of these days you might get adventurous and go out for a ride in Ladner or somewhere. You would love it. I'll take you and the bike out one day in the van."

Claire never took him up on his offer and did sell her bike right away. She must have kept the lock because there it was holding the bike tight to the side of the bin. The lock had been an old one of Jordan's; and of course, he would remember the combination. It was four numbers; they were Jan's birth year.

Jordan and Jan kept surfacing, reminding him they had once been there in person. Alive for so long in his life, creating memory after memory. All sorts of memories, good and not so good. Like a quilt, pieced together one colourful square at a time.

The piece being worked on now was soiled and torn. It needed reworking with gentle careful stitches to make it right. This piece though would stand out in Jerry's eye as the piece that hung all the others together.

His life was one so transparent, if only he would let someone grab hold of him long enough for a look. Keeping his distance and scuttling under available cover like a crab, Jerry thought he was protecting himself from discovery.

The bike has a note attached; Jerry has no plan to read it. He is sure what it says and if it did not say, get it together, it should have. Gert has been a good friend, and this was an example of Gert paying attention to his needs. About to turf the note in the trash he feels Martin's restraining hand on his wrist, "Better look inside first Jerry. Gert said it's important."

"OK I will. Thanks Martin." Jerry had not really ridden a bike in a couple of years. The last time was in Mexico and that was quite a short-lived experience with the Mexican traffic. For pedestrians trying to cross the busy roads Jerry and Jan had heard people say repeatedly that crossing was - for the quick and the dead. And for cyclists it was as bad. He and Jan had only ridden one day and when they came out of a restaurant to get their bikes, both bikes were gone.

They paid the resort they had borrowed them from at a high replacement fee. Jan had not wanted to buy insurance for the bikes; she was a bit of a cheapskate.

Stuffing the note in his coat pocket for later Jerry donned the helmet, swung his leg over the seat and rode off with a wobble down the lane. In his new community of cut throats, he would need to keep this bike safe, if he were to keep it at all.

Jerry spent the afternoon riding along one lane to the next, getting the hang of riding again. In and out, back and forth he rode until he felt confident. It was a couple of days before he felt safe enough to try out the main streets.

He had gone quite a few blocks along one of the busiest main drags, when he heard a honk behind him. Thinking he was taking up too much road and fearing a bit for his life, Jerry pulled into a gas station at Burrard Street just when his bike stopped peddling properly. Pulling in behind him was an SUV. At the same time Jerry notices his bike chain was off, he sees the young guy from the library step out of the car.

There are no coincidences Jerry; he hears Jan's voice whisper in his ear again. Jerry leans down to look at his bike chain, not having a clue how to fix it. He can feel the young guy, Geoff waiting for him to look up, so he says, "Do you know anything about bikes?"

"Ah - nope... Throw it in the back though I know someone who does. Where is your van, Pops?" "I'm not sure;

I had a bit of a problem with it." Geoff is curious but doesn't ask more. Together the two men figure out how to get the front tire off then squeeze it in the back of Geoff's SUV.

Once in the car Jerry is glad, he took the time to make friends with a skinny young punk last week. An hour ago, the same kid had given him an almost brand-new jacket. He did not even try to hit Jerry up for money. All he said was, "Hey man you could use this new jacket; it's too big for me."

Jerry took it out of the kid's hands and held it up to his body to check the fit. He had the idea the kid wanted to trade for the bike. "I don't have any money and I don't have anything to trade. Did you ever hear about Popeye's pal; cannot remember his name right now but he used to say - I'll pay you Tuesday for a hamburger today. I'd like the coat, but can I pay you later?"

"Hey, no way man I just wanted you to have it. You know that loonie you gave me last week? I put it in one of those grab machines, you know the kind that picks up toys. And I got one, pretty cool eh?"

This was turning out to be Jerry's lucky week and now his broken bike was going to get fixed with no hassle for Jerry. Luck, good or bad comes in three; this would be it for a while.

Resting his head against the back of his seat Jerry feels peaceful. The rush of riding the bike cleared a spot in his mind. A shake of his shoulder tells Jerry he fell asleep. "We're here. Dave's inside, at the back of the store - come on.

They unload the bike taking it into a bike shop and into a backroom covered with bikes in all forms of assembly. Bits and pieces lay all around the feet of a guy about Geoffrey's age. Looking up he says,

"Hey Geoffrey, long time no see. Is that your bike?"

"Hi Dave, this is...Pops. It's his bike and the chain came off; can you fix it?"

"Well of course I can fix it...for free right Geoffrey?" says Dave grinning. Pointing at Geoffrey, Dave tells Jerry that Geoffrey has never had a bike of his own to fix so he cruises the streets finding friends with broken ones. Jerry suddenly feels uncomfortable.

All the good vibes that came with the good luck he had been feeling, evaporates into mid-air. Jerry clears his throat and is about to say he can fix it himself when Dave's cell phone rings.

Hi. What's up?" The two are waiting for Dave to get off the phone, both with their hands in their pockets. Jerry hears something overhead, like a scrambling sound. Geoff sees him listening and says,

"Dave's dog, she just had pups. Hey, shall we go up and see them? There are about seven or eight pups." Pops smiles asking, "Are you sure he won't mind Geoffrey; and .... he doesn't have to fix my bike for free."

"Come on are you kidding; it's only a bike chain. Anyway, Dave owes me." Up a short flight of steps to a loft Geoff opens a door he has opened lots of times, going into what is Dave's main living area of a little bachelor pad. These days Dave spends most of his time with a woman he has hooked up with.

Dave's dog Stella lays regally stretched out with six little blond pups nursing away, her tail thumps the ground. Geoff reaches into his pocket and before bringing the treats out, he calls down to Dave

"Can Stella have a treat?"

"Oh sure. Since when, did you start carrying treats Geoff?"

"My grandmother got a dog and I'm going over there to

make friends with it a bit later. That's where I was going when Pops and I ran into each other. I hear Gran's dog is big and ferocious so thought I better bring some treats."

Handing Jerry, the treats Geoff motions for him to go forward. Stella gently takes the treats right out of Jerry's hand one after another. As the treats go in Stella's mouth Jerry gets closer and closer to the floor. By the time Dave comes up to say the bike is ready, Jerry is sitting on the floor next to the whelping box stroking one of the pups. Dave loves his dog and loves it when others pay attention to her.

"You like dogs eh Pops? She likes you too; I can tell."

Turning to Geoffrey he tells him he cannot come around later, because the guy he had lined up for puppy sitting had opted out. "You don't know anyone do you Geoffrey? I can only pay about forty bucks a night. Ideally, they absolutely must stay over. Its why the guy said no.

"He thought about it and it won't work or be worth it for him." Catching every word as he stroked Stella's neck, Jerry knows he would love to do it. Just touching the dog and her pups brings Jerry's blood pressure down. He feels himself go calm and relaxed.

"No, I don't know anyone. Unless you would like to do it, Pops, you are a bachelor aren't you? Just until Dave can find someone for tomorrow night. And look, Dave has a TV, a computer, beer..." Glancing up at the two young men he sees Dave looking hopeful and Geoff looking kind. Jerry turns back to look at Stella who wags her tail when he does.

"Sure. Why not I just lost my dog, and it has been kind of lonely. But you don't have to pay me, you fix my bike, and we'll call it even."

CHAPTER TWELVE

Dave walks with Geoff out to his car where they shake hands sharing a bit of heartfelt gratitude. Dave's happy to find someone trustworthy who will look after Stella and her pups; and Geoff feels chuffed that his friend trusts his word. And Pops has a place for the night which Geoff feels sure he would not have otherwise. Hopping in the car the first thing he does is call Dave back over to the window and suggest he put some food in his fridge and tell Jerry to help himself.

"The guys a bit down on his luck. He doesn't take care of himself; you know how it is." Next, he calls Dixie, and leaves a voice message to tell her he found the man with the van, Mr. Landvik. He adds that he is going to his Gran's to meet her new dog and will be home after that. Voice mail picked up, so he left a message.

Pulling into the back lane of his Gran's place, he catches sight of her throwing a ball repeatedly up into the air. The porch light illuminates her action on this beautifully clear November night. There it goes again. The ball sails up into the air but this time Gran does not catch it. Letting it fall and bounce across the ground as a surprisingly small dog chased after it. Dixie said Gran's dog was big and ferocious; this small one is more like it.

Geoffrey, leaning over the top of the fence says, "Hey Gran; cute dog." When he comes through the gate the little dog runs over and begins circling Geoffrey's legs. He barks as he goes running faster and faster. Watching him Mavis is reminded of a story book she had when she was a kid called - Little Black Sambo. Not a popular particularly politically correct book for this period in history, but it had been a favourite for Mavis.

Jack is wearing a blue and white argyle sweater to keep him warm. The sweater, white wiry hair and the slight black eye patch makes him look like a dog stepping out of a calendar shoot, quite the spoiled pooch already. Once in the house, Jack will not stand still to have his sweater off, so he can go flake out on a sheep skin next to the sectional. Geoffrey watches his Gran closely. It is Geoffrey's opinion, there is something sad about a single woman doting on a dog.

Gran looks different but Geoffrey cannot put his finger on it. One thing is certain though the dog is giving his grandmother a purpose. Spotting her throwing the ball up in the air, grinning and laughing aloud at her dog had been surprising for Geoffrey to see.

He guessed some people really do benefit from a pet. Like Pops today, sitting patting Stella and her pups. He wonders how Pops is going to make out with Stella overnight. And wonders too, if he will end up filling in for Dave over the next week or so. Sometimes Geoffrey wonders if his choice of profession is right for him. Sorting people and their needs out is what delivers real satisfaction to Geoffrey. Knowing he acted as facilitator or a part of a personal process that is what makes him tick.

"Hey Gran, did I tell you I met an old guy at the library? I have seen him around a few different places but today I helped him out with his bike chain...He is a dog lover too. Anyway, I saw him earlier and I was just thinking when I watched you and Jack play, maybe you'd like to meet him?"

"Meet him? Why would I?" This was not the reaction Geoffrey was looking for. Dixie told him that rumour had it his Gran had been dumped by a man she had just met. Big indicator she is ready to have a relationship. Embarrassed, Geoffrey says, "I don't know. I just thought maybe you might like to date now that Stan has been gone awhile."

Mavis gives Geoffrey a sidelong look, sizing him up imagining his motivation had been a prod from Dixie. "Look Geoffrey, I am already interested in someone so that's that. Sorry. Besides, - Stan has been gone a long time at least that is how I feel; I got lonely but now that I have Jack, I'm not so lonely.

"You know the girls think of me as a desperate old lady. They act as if my trotting over to make dinner and giving them money from time to time is some sort of favour to me. But Geoffrey all I want is to do something nice and to have purpose. It's what we all want isn't it?

"I guess for women it might be different. I do not know what men want; but I do need and want to have purpose and feel as if I add value to another life. Now I have a dog to take care of; one who sure keeps me happy and entertained." Laughing at herself, Mavis smiles and takes Geoffrey's slim face between her tiny hands and says,

"No Geoffrey, I don't want to date. I want to allow a relationship to flow out of nowhere. Let it wash over me like a welcome rain. One that just happens as if it were meant to be - but not a set up..." Letting go of his face seeing the same look in her grandson's eyes as she always did when she let go his cheeks.

Taking hold of his face again, she leans on toes up toward him then tilts his head down; a light kiss on the forehead followed by another on his lips. This she has done since he was a baby. To kiss his lovely face and to have her welcoming kiss received was theirs. A shared moment every time they met.

She wonders if it is the person who is missed when they are gone or if it is these small routines and traditions. The soup, the chat, and the kiss all something they share more often as two. Geoffrey never shy or awkward to avoid what he wanted even when he had friends about; their time was not complete without her final seal and his returning kiss and hug.

Stan, bless his heart had left them to their own devices while grandmother instructed her boy in various things. He learned how to play hide and seek, to make muffins, to re-attach buttons. He learned how to use the sewing machine and to crochet a dish cloth. She taught him to iron her linen dinner napkins, how to hem pants... All skills Mavis said every person - male or female - should know before they set out to find a life.

And after every lesson Mavis caught the boy before he left to give him a kiss. When he was a baby her lips grazed his head lightly before he went to sleep. Sometimes blowing air out her lips against him like a gentle breeze helped his eyes flutter shut.

Each time she plants that kiss, the wave of other ages and stages swim into her vision. His little body lying in her arms, the toddler trying to escape, a boy convinced she knew it all as if by magic, another who came to her with trouble and now this young man; bending his head knowing he is recipient of all she has. Her grandson is so much loved by her; a boy her own daughter pushed aside.

Mavis takes Geoffrey into the kitchen doing what she always does when he is not staying for soup. She packs some up in a yogurt container for him to take home. Looking up at him watching her speculatively she feels a slight shift in the atmosphere. The ground she has feet firmly on is now shifting beneath her; she does not know where she stands with Geoffrey.

Does he judge her for thinking of sharing her life again? To smooth things over between them, as it is true Mavis is prone to do especially when Geoffrey bids her goodbye. Wanting to stretch out their time together today she says, "Tell me about this friend of yours Geoffrey? What's his name for starters and what do you have in common with an old guy?"

"Well, he is smart - like me - for starters. He likes research and is a researcher. So, we have that in common. We both like to go camping and the outdoors. He has an interest in ..." and here Geoffrey stops. He never found out what happened to the van. "You know what Gran I have to get going it's getting late."

"But what's his name?"

"Oh yeah... he told me to call him Pops. I guess that is why I wanted you two to meet. I miss Stan - my real Pops. But this guy, Pops... he is nothing like Stan. He is more complex and actually – well I don't know his story yet. But when I do, I'll tell you Gran. Give me the soup, and don't walk me out, it's too dark now and I gotta fly." This time its Geoffrey who kissed his grandmother, right on the top of her head, a new routine.

A CYCLIST at full speed runs a red light. He is carrying two full black garbage bags across his back. The SUV just misses him as he sails by; Geoff sees the whites of the guy's eyes when he turns his skeletal head to make sure of something behind him. Limping along to keep up with the bike, an old black dog is giving a bit more speed; trying to keep up and get across to safety in time.

All traffic is slowed or stopped and the dog dodges between the cars, scanning the distance to catch sight of his master. Having a change of mind about going home, Geoff finds himself turning off the road and heads to the bike shop. All the front lights are out but he can see a glow of life in the back. Approaching by the lane on foot with the soup in hand, he is about to knock on the door when he sees it edging open.

"Geoff, you're back? This is a busy place; Dave came back too. You just missed him. It seems like he isn't sure I will be OK. It'll be a surprise if he doesn't return again to check up on things."

"How did you know it was me and not a burglar?" Pointing to an area under the roof Pops says, "Dave's got a camera set up to a screen in the workshop." Pops swings the door wide for his new friend Geoff, to step inside. "I want to show you something." The two men head to the very back corner of the shop. Geoff instinctively knows what he is going to be shown.

Opening the Men's Room door exposes walls that are covered with photos of VW vans of all years. Turning to Geoff, his friend has a huge smile on his face. His eyes have lost the deadened glaze. They have returned to clear and bright and the bluest blue - like his mother's.

"That's one of the reasons I came back, I was going to ask, where is your van? Parked under cover I hope." The light went out, in both the bathroom and in the man's eyes. Following Pops out and up the steps to the loft, with his Gran's soup in hand he is almost speechless at the change in his friend. "Oh, before I forget my Gran makes the best soup. Here I brought you some."

"No need to give me your soup Geoff. Look what Dave brought - a whole bag of groceries; but he did ask if I would stay until the weekend. I'm sure I can." Holding out his hand Pops takes the soup setting it on the counter.

"Tell you what. Stay and have some soup with me. Dave brought a loaf of some hardy looking bread and some cheese." Geoff looked at his cell phone, to check the time. "Oh, you probably have to be somewhere right? Bet you've got a girl friend?"

"Nope... I don't have to be somewhere. But yes, I do have a girl friend and I ought a give her a quick call to let her know I'll be late. I'll stay for soup but only if you tell me about your van." Hesitating long enough to gauge a response before stepping away, Geoff opens the door and down the steps for a bit of privacy. And he wants to get something out of his car.

Dixie still is not answering; he leaves a new message and sends a text too. She is bound to pick up one or the other. He props the door open with a bike tire, grabs the book out of the car, then heads back upstairs to share some food with Pops. He can smell the soup when he walks in. Stella can too and is sitting at her new friend's leg waiting for handouts. Why is it that people are more likely to give a handout to a dog than to another person?

Pops looks right at home here. Stella clearly has him pegged as the guy with the food but before they sit down to

137

eat Pops says, "I need to take Stella out to relieve herself; be right back. Don't touch anything."

Geoff is not too sure what he means by that but when Pops comes back up the stairs the first thing, he sees is Geoff stirring the pot. Shaking his head in annoyance Pops pulls the drawers open looking for cutlery, finally spotting some in a coffee mug beside the sink.

"OK - let's eat." Stella goes back to her pups somehow suspecting there would be none for her. Circling twice, she lays down and turns one of the pups over with the side of her nose and begins licking under the little guy's tail. Geoff knows what is happening and almost loses his appetite. The familiar scent of his grandmother's soup wafts under his nose encouraging him to eat.

The bread and soup almost gone; Geoff stands to clear the table. Again, Pops looks a bit miffed. "What's up Pops I'm just doing what comes natural. Don't you like help?"

"No, I actually don't like help when I'm cooking. I don't know why I'm like that; tonight though, I wanted to give you a thank you." Looking down into his empty bowl for a beat, Pops says, "You must know I'm homeless. When I took a shower in Dave's washroom even I, could see an old man who hasn't had a bath for a while. And I haven't been sleeping rough all that long; only a week or maybe two...not much more."

"You don't need to thank me Pops; we are on our way to a good friendship and this is how it all starts. At least that is what my Gran would say. She told me today a relationship needs to just happen.

She believes in magic, my Gran does. Everything happening for a reason, a season, or a lifetime she says. And because I spend so much time in her company, I guess it makes no matter if my friends are my age or your age. I do care if we have something of interest in common though.

"And Pops - I don't have many actual friends." This Pops finds hard to believe but the grandmother sounds genuine enough. Pops thinks he might like to meet her some day; he would let her know what a fine grandson she has.

Tapping Pops on the back of his hand, Geoff continues, "I don't have many friends but that doesn't mean I'm lonely or don't know many people. What I mean is, I am selective about who I call my lifetime friends. I pick them with care. Someone like you, we have something in common; something to build on. Plus, we keep bumping into each other. And there are no coincidences Pops."

Geoff reaches down to pull the VW van book out from under his chair. Pops almost bolts again when he sees it but remains in his seat completely frozen; he has no will to move. Flipping through the pages of the book Geoff finds the familiar photo of Jan with son Jordan beside the VW van and says, "After I left you here today I remembered I had this book to take back to the library. I was going to drop it off after going to my Gran's.

"But then a guy riding a bike, right in front of me reminded me of you. The guy I saw looked like he had been riding a bike all his life and you..." Pops interrupts.

"I look like I'm still on training wheels. Yeah, I know. A good friend gave me the bike the other day; she thought it might help to get me out of my own God damned head." Geoff knows from a workshop on active listening that this is when paraphrasing back is helpful. Instead he says nothing.

The first to talk often ends the conversational direction – this is something his Gran once told him. So, he listens as Pops opens-up about all that has happened to him after the day at the library. Unleashed too is the agony of the last four years and it feels surprisingly good to talk about it.

They sit together on the couch with the book open on Pop's lap. Stella stands facing them as if sensing she is needed. Her head shifting back and forth while an old man talks, and a young man listens. Geoff does not try to gauge how Pop feels; he hears it in a voice that's either filled with emotion or full of cold self-protective denial.

Geoff hears about a son who sounds like he was adored by his father. He hears about a son who rejects his father for years until he is ill. And even then, it is the closeness of his mother, the son, Jordon wanted. He hears about a son more interested in remembering and repeating the story of one failed vacation than remembering all the other holidays – happy holidays, they all shared.

To Geoff's ear it sounds like his new friend is trying to rebound from and rewrite the history that brought him face to face with grief. Don't speak ill of the dead is something he had heard his Gran say. Taking the book off Pops lap and setting it on the coffee table Geoff stands. With nothing to offer and drained of emotion Pops has nothing left to say.

Geoff asks again, "But what happened to your van?" Geoff's aware, in a way he must sound uncaring, but he sees a direct link between what had been, what could have been, and what is to Pops a real disaster.

Pops tells him about the day he is mugged. They had just run into each other at the downtown library. Pointing at the coffee table he reminds Geoff he had that book with him.

It is the photo in the book that set him into a state of high emotion and panic that day. He retells a painful story about the van theft, the break in at his landlady's house. He tells how later the same night; he woke up in the hospital. There were two cops in his room waiting to take a statement.

And then the long wait while his van eventually is found across the line in Bellingham. Pops avoids saying what condition he fears the van is in. He avoids thinking about it or saying the words as if words will seal the demise of the van permanently making it all too real. A single tear rolls out the corner of Pop's eye.

"Maybe I can help you with something Pops. Just tell me what you need, it might help. Two heads can be better than one; am I right? Come on; tell me why you don't get the van?" Rough hands, dirt filled lined and stained hands. Hands that once had been the softies of a man not used to physical work, add strength to his story.

Hands open wide, fingers splayed; he runs them through thick white hair that lays in waves a top a big head. Rubbing his eyes with those same dirt riddled fingers he steadies himself so he can say, "The thieves took it to a garage and got long term parking. My wallet got stolen my entire ID so no driver's license.

"What little money I had, was in the wallet. So, it is in a car park waiting for someone to come down there and get it and I don't have any money to retrieve it.

"There I said it. It will eventually be sold. I know I need to get ready for that or to find a buyer. Geoff all the memories I just told you about. They will be gone with the van. I won't have anything left at all. Apparently, the guy at the garage wants first crack at buying it though."

Stella is back with her pups, keeping a steady eye on her new friend. Rising Jerry stands beside the whelping box. His hands stuck deep in his pockets. He rocks his body slightly, turning his head to look at Geoff.

"Unless you'd be interested in buying it?"

CHAPTER THIRTEEN

Pops promises, the next day he will check on the fees and storage costs. Geoff makes a promise of his own, to drive Pop down to Bellingham to get the van.

"They stole my driver's license Geoffrey. I have not applied for a new one yet. I can't drive it without a license, and I can't get across the border without a passport. The passport, luckily, is in the van right where I hid it."

"Oh man," says Geoffrey, "it's getting more and more complicated isn't it? Have you talked to the guy at the garage Pops?

"No, I haven't. But Claire, the lawyer I told you about? Her assistant Lynn has been doing all the phoning and talking. I've got her number but haven't called her yet." Taking his two hands Geoff digs them into his thick curls turning them into a tangled mess with one ruffle.

"OK Pops... call this Lynn person. Ask her to contact the garage where your van is; they can at least check to see if your passport is where you think it is. If it is, ask that they courier it up here...to Dave's. Oh, and ask her to find out how much the impound fees and so on are? We'll need to know that, to get it back." It looked like Jerry was given another piece of luck when Geoff had turned up behind him the other morning.

DAVE IS VISIBLY pleased that Jerry had cleaned the entire whelping box and given Stella her morning food and exercise. They were just coming back when Dave pulled up on his bike. Taking the leash from Pops he takes Stella for another walk around the block. When he got back inside, he smelt coffee and went on up to the loft before opening the shop.

"Hey, you cleaned out the whelping box, good job. Thanks man: I was going to do that when I came in." Looking around the big open room he notes that Jerry cleaned the whole place and organized everything, since yesterday afternoon. Papers in recycling, dishes done, everything looked neat.

"Can I ask you something Pops?"

"Sure, go ahead."

"How do you know Geoffrey, and where do you live? Do you even have a place to stay? What is your story man? "The confidence that was building in Jerry, evaporates as he realizes he's getting the heave ho. Measuring his words in his usual slow and calculated way he doesn't get a chance before Dave says,

"Because if you do not have anywhere to be, like for a week or two, it would help me out to have you stay here… You don't have to stay with Stella all the time. Just at night and even then, man, she can be on her own for a few hours at a time. But I need someone I can trust with her. She's my girl. And I will pay you of course like I said, but I can only manage forty bucks a night."

To this generous offer Pops says, "Sounds good Dave and thanks. As it happens, I am between places; this helps me out. You can pay me but only a hundred bucks for the week. And if you think you trust me can you pay me up front?" Over the next couple of hours Dave gets to know a bit more about Jerry and vice versa.

Dave and his girlfriend are on and off again and right now they are on, so he spends a lot of time at her place. But taking Stella to live at Alisha's is out of the question as far as her landlord's concerned. Dave's place is way too small and junky for Alisha. But they might move in together in which case Stella will come too.

While they get to know each other Pops moves around the bike repair area doing what he likes to do most; create order. Pretty soon, Pops is upstairs back to Stella and to use Dave's phone.

LYNN'S GRATIFIED by the call; to hear his voice shows he has it together enough to get in touch himself. So far, it is Gert calling or Claire asking if she had heard from him. Both women would happily have retrieved the van, but it was only a proxy or the Van's owner who could do so. Gert felt certain Jerry would and should sell his van. He needed the money more than he needed to hang on to it; or so thought Gert.

Claire though knew he needed the van even more than the money. With the van he had shelter, self-respect and all his history right under his feet. Gert felt with the cash he could buy some dignity and self-respect. Gert did not like herself for it, but she had lost patience with Jerry. The only one who knows where Jerry can be found is Lynn and she is now sworn to secrecy.

The only person Lynn's got permission to give Jerry's address to is the owner of the garage where the van is being kept. Instead of sending the passport via courier though, it gets hand delivered by the Bellingham garage owner, Melvin.

MELVIN, keen to buy the van feels sure by introducing himself he will charm his way into striking a deal. He asks Lynn to let Mr. Landvik know he plans to be there in four hours. Lynn gets Dave on the line when she calls the number Jerry left earlier.

In her confusion when she hears a younger voice say she has reached a cycle shop, she almost says, "Wrong number," but instead she asks can she leave a message for the owner of a VW van, a Mr. Landvik. After the initial confusion Dave writes down the message assuring her, he will pass it on.

Before passing the message on to Pops, he steps into the back lane and leaves a quick voice mail for Geoffrey. Earlier Geoff called to brief him on what has been going on. He had checked in with Dave to see if there might be a spot for the van to stay under cover for a few days. "Jeeze I don't know Geoffrey...it's kind of tight in here. I'll see what I can do; it'll only be a day or two...right?"

Disconnecting and back inside Dave calls up to Pops who appears at the top of the steps cradling a pup close to his chest. Stella is at his side eyeing him with suspicion; she wants her pup back. Dave relays the message about Melvin bringing the passport himself.

When Pops asks why he cannot come earlier Dave says, "He just has a few ends to tie up but says he will be here by 3:30 at the latest. But can you be here Pops? He wants to give the passport directly to you. I suspect he will try to talk you into selling him the van.

"Up to you Pops but Lynn says she did a bit of research... and your van - depending on its shape could bring anywhere from a low twenty thousand to a high of forty or fifty thousand. Is it still in mint condition? Cause if it is Pops that fifty thousand could be yours."

"Well I don't think it's in Mint condition but fairly good condition ...exceptionally good condition, actually. Good to know Dave." And back into the loft he goes. Jerry has four hours; he has time to go to Mrs. J's house. He needs to check for mail if he wants to get a new license. But he does not want to take a chance he will miss this Melvin character. Pops supposes he can do what Geoff suggests and let him drive it back but then who would drive them both to pick it up?

Too many uncertainties; Jerry needs to get his license. Making a snap decision, he gets on his bike to see if there is any mail for him at Mrs. J's. If there is, he will go to the nearest licensing office. He is sure the one in the East End is the closest to his old address.

Five minutes after he leaves, Geoff calls. He had not listened to the messages, but Dave fills him in. "I can't be there by four Dave. I'm still at work, then I've gotta submit a paper. The earliest I can get there today is 5:30 or 6. Can you just stand close by when they're talking?

"Let me know what the guy says OK? The truth is, if the van gets sold, I'd like to be the one to buy it. When you see it, you'll know why? It's everything I've ever wanted and a place to make my own memories."

Dave knows how transient Geoff's childhood was. That is how and why he met Geoffrey. Geoff started at the same school as Dave in grade seven. He was only there for a couple of months and then moved on. They ran into each other again in grade eight when Geoff went to live with his grandparents for a while. All of grade eight Geoffrey's dad worked out of town so he and Dave lived just a few blocks apart. The catchment area being larger for a high school, Geoff was able to stay at the same school until graduation. Geoff had moved around so much he felt rootless now.

One time when he was about seven or eight, shortly after his Gran married Stan, he was taken out for the day with Stan to see an old pal of his. The pal lived in a van in a trailer park in Surrey. Or at least his van was parked there for a few days until he made his way back across a couple of provinces to Saskatchewan where he lived. He showed Geoff around then made them all lunch on an outdoor camp stove.

After lunch and a game of cards, the vans bed was made up and a young Geoff was told to go in the van and have a nap. A little old for napping, instead, Geoff lay on the bed making plans to have a van of his own someday. Outside the van, the two men talked, and Geoff listened about the travels the van had been on, adding to Geoffrey's fantasy. That day was one of the best Geoff ever had with Stan and it was the one of two days he ever spent with Stan on his own, without his Gran with them. And the van? It was a '65 Classic VW Van with a pop-up roof.

MAVIS DRIES her hands on the towel. She looks down into the beady little dark eyes of her pooch who is standing right next to her legs. She can count on him to be close by wherever she is in the little house. Mavis asks, "Is this the day I can leave you on your own Jack? The dog book says I should get you in the habit of being on your own. I just don't like to leave you. Tell you what. Let's go for a walk first - then I'll go out. And you won't." For an answer Jack wagged his tail and ran in circles all the way to the door.

Before she goes though, she is going to give Gert a call at the store. As happy as she is with her little dog Mavis wants Jerry to be with them too. They are a package. She saw them as a trio in her fantasy that first day on her bus ride home from Doreen's and that is what she wants.

Never in her life has she felt so clear. She still hears Jerry shouting, "Jack off, Jack off." And this makes her laugh out loud. Every time she thinks of him in his dirty jacket trying to herd the little dog as Jack is dancing just out of reach, she smiles. Her hand on the phone, ready to dial, it rings. Picking it up she says, "Hello."

And for the next ten minutes she hears some news that changes the world of her two daughters. It is a call from the hospital. Robin has developed infection after infection; he got pneumonia and died in his sleep three nights before.

Mavis is told the hospital does not have contact information for the daughter who had popped by from time to time or numbers for any of Robin's other relatives or if he had any. One of his union brothers though had left his number when he paid a visit.

When the hospital contacted him as a last resort, he was able to find Mavis's name listed as Robin's beneficiary and next of kin on a union insurance policy. Feeling shock and relief, Mavis replaces the telephone receiver. Even after all these years the mere mention of Robin's name sends chills of fear and anger up her spine.

Both girls take it well and both have the crass to ask if he left them anything. When Mavis hears them ask the same question, one after the other a very frosty front moves in between Mavis and her daughters. How had she raised such mercenaries; she has no idea. Robin never remarried saying to all who would listen, "Once was enough."

She hopes Robin had been smart enough to leave a clearly written will, so the girls do not have to wade through the details of probate. They certainly are not equipped for that. But it is not up to Mavis. For the moment she plans stay out of it.

"Oh, I don't know; I told your sister you'll have to follow that up yourselves. I am sure; if he has a will or any assets to leave, you'll both be named. But why didn't you leave your number with the hospital?" She asked both girls. The body had been at the morgue for three days.

The death certificate all signed. It is Bethany who asks if Mavis will take care of the cremation. "I mean pay for it and everything and write a notice for the paper? Could you maybe have a little do at your house. Just for family?"

"Sorry Bethany, but you girls will need to take care of the cremation and cost yourselves. And no, I won't have a little do at my house. I'll help with food and such but not at my house. It would be more appropriate at your place dear, or at Doreen's. What does Doreen say about it, did you ask her?"

Mavis is not about to mention anything about the insurance policy, and she might never mention it. Her plan is to divide the money between the grandchildren putting an equal amount in trust for each.

She will give Geoffrey his now, but Charlene will wait to use her portion for university. According to Ricki, university is the direction Charlene is best suited for. The little boys so far did not look like university material. Further education of some sort would be a help in their future.

Mavis is deep in thought about all these things, when out of the corner of her eye she watches the last light of the day die in the west. She puts a call in to the crematorium to give them Bethany's number, goes ahead and writes a short obituary, leaves Geoffrey a voice mail to call her and now it is too late in the day to give Jack a chance to be at home alone.

Surprising after this long draining day she feels nothing at all except the fatigue she always feels after navigating phone calls with either daughter. She does not care that Robin's dead; he had been dead to her for years.

When Geoffrey hears the news about his maternal grandfather it is from Doreen. She called all the library's until she found him. The tears she weeps over the phone, Geoffrey finds hard to believe are for Robin.

Before she says goodbye, she asks the unbelievable and he knows he was right. He knew it was all about Doreen as usual when she said, "Geoffrey Babe, I wonder if you could find out if he left a will? Do you know how to do that Geoffrey? You're so good with computers and you know how to go hunting around the internet for stuff...any ideas?" As it happens, he has none. He tells her, "call a lawyer." As an afterthought he says, "sorry for your loss." And disconnects.

IT IS FOUR PM, so he knows he missed Melvin from Bellingham. Dixie picks up right away when she sees its Geoffrey; she is hoping they can see each other for dinner. When she hears his news and his plans, she understands she will be solo again tonight. Dixie would be ticked off if it were young guys keeping Geoffrey out till all hours. But it never is.

He is a helper of humans, her Geoffrey is. That's what Dixie's sisters called him. They say, "How's the little helper of humans doing today"? Especially Bonnie, she never got why he was so thrilled about computer science when it was people who made him tick.

His hope of being a professor would give him both, but Bonnie still did not get it. Dixie is finished for the day. She has no clients and nowhere to be, so decides to go home and snuggle up with a good book.

Picking up her cell once more before heading to her place, she phones a florist and sends a bouquet to Geoffrey's mother and aunt. She sends one to Mavis as well for having to put up with all she did.

HIS PHONE BEEPS with another message. He gets so many he rarely listens to most of them. If it is his mother Doreen calling, he won't call back and erases her message before he even listens to it. If he sees his Gran's number, he calls her back, to find out what she needs; same with any of his friend's numbers.

So, when he sees Dave's missed call, he does not bother listening to the message, he just hits the number and calls back as he drives.

"Geoff." Dave enthuses, "How's it going my man?"

"Hey Dave, sorry I missed your call; how did it go today? Did Melvin turn up?"

"Yup. He's still here. They're upstairs having a beer together like a couple of old friends. I looked a while ago and they're pouring over some VW photos in a book Pops has up there. Melvin plans to stay over.

"Not here though Geoff. With a friend in Vancouver and says he can drive Pops or as he calls him Mr. Landvik, to his van tomorrow. But I gotta tell you Geoff, he never got his license today. Not even a temporary one. He said the lineup was so long he had to leave to get back here or miss Melvin."

"Do you think I should swing by? He hasn't agreed to sell the van, has he?"

"Nope. Ah, sorry Geoff, I overheard him say he's going to go on title with his grandson and give it to him outright eventually." This is news to Geoff. When they talked last night Pops never mentioned a grandson. His son Jordan was gay. But he supposed he did not know everything about Pops or Jordan for that matter. Disappointed and relieved Pops has no plan to sell; Geoff wonders how he can at least get to ride in the van.

"Tell Pops not to worry. I'll go with him tomorrow if Melvin doesn't mind me tagging along. Then I'll drive us back in the van. Do you think he'll let me drive it?" Dave's laughter makes Geoff laugh too. "Tell Pops I'll be by after I drop off my paper at the U."

WHEN HE RETURNS his Grandmother's phone call, he hears cutlery and knows she is clearing a solo dinner setting, off the table. "Hi Gran, I see you tried calling me earlier; was it about Robin? Doreen tracked me down at a library and told me. But are you OK?" This last question makes Mavis smile.

Only Geoffrey would ask, is she ok. Even though she has not seen Robin in over twenty years he would imagine she somehow still cared for him. Mavis does not want to burst

Geoffrey's bubble by saying - you don't know how many times I wished he would keel over. Instead, in a soft voice she thanked him for his thoughtfulness.

Asking solicitously how his mother was holding up. Geoffrey never told his Gran what he thought about his grandfathers' death or about Doreen's reaction to it either. They were two birds of a feather. Each wanting to spare the other from seeing the raw under belly of ugliness. Or so they thought.

Each wanted the other to have an opinion and to this end, neither was completely honest. Taking a bit of a risk, Mavis decides to tell him about the insurance.

"Geoffrey, I have something on my mind. Can I tell you in confidence?"

"Sure Gran. What's up?" Geoffrey asks, trying for casually, flippant – nonchalance; even though he feels intrigue. His Gran never asks him to keep a confidence. "Did your mother tell you it was me who was contacted with the news your grandfather had passed away?"

"Nope."

"Doreen never left a number...or should I say there was no contact number for Doreen and somehow the hospital found my name as next of kin. Well someone from his work looked in his file and saw me listed as next of kin and this is the part I want kept in confidence. I am named as beneficiary on at least one policy."

"Really? Wow that's great gran." Geoffrey feels giddy with excited anticipation of Doreen finding out. It will serve her right. "Does Doreen know, or Bethany?"

"Oh, my goodness no... I never told them. And I will tell you Geoffrey I'm just not sure what I want to do with the money yet, but I have a bit of a plan."

"You know what Gran? Robin was a jerk. You deserve the

money; that is the nicest thing he ever did for you. He wanted you to have it."

"Nice of you to say Geoffrey - but I'll tell you something else. One day last year you told me your mother Doreen, is an S disturber? She got that from her dad. I feel bad about speaking ill of the dead and it might be the wine but now that he is gone, I feel a relief as big as a house."

"How much have you been drinking Gran?" Geoffrey had never heard his grandmother speaking so candidly before and he imagines the shock of Robin dropping dead called for a drink." "Yes, I had a glass of wine and am just about to have another. Do I sound drunk?" Asks Mavis, appalled with herself that she is sounding a bit tipsy.

"Geoffrey, before I let you go can I ask you another favour?"

"Sure, Gran anything."

"The girls want a party for Robin at Doreen's on the weekend. I am doing most of the cooking. Can you bring Charlene over here Friday night? She asked if she could come here to help me. And she will need a ride with all the food on Sunday - to your mum's. You'll go with Charlene, won't you Geoffrey? And Dixie too?"

"Sure Gran. To both things. I will get Charlene and bring her along to your place; I wanted to see her anyway. See you Friday." By the time Geoffrey hung up he was at the University. He could have stopped by his grandmother's en-route and feels a bit of guilt that he did not when she was just a few blocks out of his way. Next time he promised himself. Tonight, though he wants to see Pops and make sure he is doing OK.

CHAPTER FOURTEEN

Pops is on top of the world. Melvin walks in holding up a set of keys on a chain Jerry has never seen before until he takes a closer look and recognizes the well-worn keys. They dangle from a brand-new key chain with a giant shiny VW on it. His own key chain had a smaller VW, backed by an oval piece of worn leather. Right in the middle of the leather is a small picture of him holding a baby.

Jordan is in one arm and the other arm is wrapped around the shoulder of his young wife. That key chain is all part of the history that held him together these few years. Jerry surprised himself by feeling nothing at all when Melvin said the thieves still had the price tag on the new key chain.

As if preforming a magic trick, out of his front shirt pocket Melvin tugs the old familiar looking key chain. "Is this one yours then?" Melvin says with a smile coupled with a big slap on the back. Jerry sees right away Melvin's a jester and just shakes his head; taking the keys he transfers them to the old chain. Melvin hands his passport over too and when Jerry offers him a beer, of course Melvin says, "You bet Buddy there's nothing better than Canadian beer!"

At first Jerry thinks this Melvin guy is like any other stereotypical brash American he has met in his travels. Pretty soon he warms to the man as they talk about V Dubs as Melvin likes to call them. Jerry learns there are V Dub Clubs all over North America, not just the one he and Jan had belonged to.

"And they have V Dub owner camping conventions too. People lining up to buy the '65 Classic and almost willing to pay, any price, Jerry. And especially for one in such good condition as yours; I took the liberty of checking a few things and mechanically it is in excellent shape. And the body is in near mint condition."

Melvin is persuasive in marketing himself as a perfect V Dub owner. But before things go too far, Jerry tells a small white lie just to put an end to the sales pitch. Jerry worries that he might be persuaded during his time of need.

He knows if he can make it another couple of months, he will be fine. The envelope that Gert attached to the bike had a CPP application attached. Surprising himself he filled it out and took it right in. There's another form for surviving spouse pension, he filled that in too and was able to find a copy of the death certificate, his marriage certificate, and his birth certificate in a box he had asked Mrs. Bergen to store awhile back.

Gert's note said she had taken the liberty of getting a change of address form for him as well. She said he could use her address for the apartment above the store until he got a permanent address of his own.

These were steps he ought to have taken long ago but the familiar push from Gert and of having the forms was the final boost he needed. Things seemed to be falling into place. All he has left to do now is deal with the van.

GEOFF DRIVES up just as Pops waves goodbye to a bulky guy behind the wheel of a sleek sedan as it drove off in the opposite direction down the lane. When Geoff got out of his SUV he was greeted by a merry man.

Pops had a twinkle in his eye, and he looked like he had just found a million bucks. "Geoff you're back. You just missed Melvin he brought my passport and the keys to my van."

"Dave told me he was here. And he said you couldn't get your license today because the lineup was too long?"

"Yup. Come on let's go inside. I want to show you something."

Inside and upstairs they go. Once in the little apartment Pops kneels beside the whelping box. Tenderly he lifts one of the pups and holds it out to Geoff. Not sure what Pops has in mind he takes the pup. Bending down for another there they stand each with a ball of fur in their hands. Pops nudges Geoff with his arm holding his pup at eye level.

"See this pup? Look Geoff, her eyes are open. All the pups have their eyes open now. Isn't that amazing? While Melvin was here; well since early this morning, I've watched them as their eyes began to open; one pup after another. But it took all day for them to go from closed to open and it was a slow process.

"That's how I feel. Like I have not been seeing clearly for a while, until today. Today Melvin brought me hope. I'm elated - elevated in fact. I feel as if this old man has been in the dark. And now, I understand something clearly at last. I feel so full as if I've been dusted off and given a second chance. I know exactly what I am going to do, not how I will do it. But I know what I'll do. The first step is to get my van back."

Geoff has not heard Pops string so many words together in the brief time he is known the man. The moment seems so monumental he doesn't know what he can add so he settles for a way to help Pops reach part of his dream and asks, "Want me to come with you tomorrow to get the van?"

"Yes, I do Geoffrey. There are only two problems. I don't have the money to get my van out of hawk and I told a bit of a lie to Melvin so he wouldn't talk me into selling."

"Don't worry Pops; I'm fairly sure I can help you out with the money part. What lie did you tell though?"

"I said you were my grandson." Geoff laughed and threw his arm around the shoulder of the older man; then laughed some more. The two men stand for a while longer each holding a pup. Geoff remembers Dixie at home alone and decides he would like to join her.

Placing the pup back with its litter mates Geoff is about to walk toward the door when a thought occurs to him and he asks, "Hey Pops I guess this means I get to drive your van tomorrow?"

"Under caution - yes Geoff - under extreme caution. You will be the fourth person to drive it; my son never even drove it. Not once, he did not want to. When I think back, I wonder if Jordan was jealous of the van. I guess I might have spent more time with the van than with him.

"For years I imagined a father figure, was what he hoped to find with another man. One time, the time in that photo taken just before he and his mother went on a trip together. Just the two of them; I was not invited or wanted along by either of them. Jordan and I never went on any trips together, just the two of us. But that's the thing I know now; I missed my opportunity to ask. He didn't come with me. He never once asked to do a trip alone with me.

"I never asked him to join me on a trip either. Too much pride, I guess. Earlier tonight I wondered why it is, some men do not ask for what they need most. I never got the answer but guess what Geoffrey? Tonight, is the first time I have ever asked for what I need. I asked you; you said yes, it was so easy.

"Now go home and remember what I just said. Life is full of opportunity; you need to have your eyes open to know it when it is right in front of you; to take advantage. Keep your eyes open and if you can, do not miss a single opportunity. Live your life with awareness."

GEOFFREY SEES a reading light on in their upstairs suite. The silhouette of Dixie in the window seat with a book stands out like a beacon of welcome. Putting the car into park he keeps his eyes open and watches her read. Taking this opportunity to see and recognize the lovely vision of Dixie's silhouette.

Going out to the sidewalk he passes the other cars lined up along the street. White balls of a snow berry bush glow by the streetlights shine. With care he snaps off some of the branches of Dixie's dearly loved late autumn flower.

She will be surprised he remembers they are a favourite. But how can he forget a word she says, a gesture she makes. Geoffrey feels the same way about opportunity as Pops does. Knowing the time taken to cultivate a friendship with Pops was an opportunity to know someone with a common interest and already they were both benefiting.

And Dixie, when she sees the snow berries, she will know her needs are near to his thoughts. Holding the twigs of white berries forth it is this bundle of sticks that she sees first as he comes through the door. Geoffrey hears the delightful sigh of Dixie as she swoons over his small offering.

How did he get so lucky to have someone so good? Seeing her quietly reading, knowing she has been watching for his car. Reaching for her hand he pulls her up and out of the window seat.

She comes easily to him so he can hold her in his arms. Today he is grateful he took the time to step out of his youthful self-absorption; that was an opportunity. To see life beyond Geoffrey's own needs held its own rewards.

FIRST THING in the morning Pops is up, showered, and ready to roll. He cannot get over the fact that his life is feeling almost smooth and steady. A roof over his head gives him time to take a breath, to see a life full of potential. The advice from Gert to seek grief counselling is his next step.

No longer having the business card of the psychologist he found the day he saw Jack and Mavis was of little concern. Feeling able to reach out on his own to seek support, was like a shot of power right into his arm. He better get to a telephone and give Gert a call. She will have heard he picked up the bike.

Using Dave's desk phone, he dials *67 to block the number he calls Gert from. He hopes to protect Dave from a whole slew of people bothering him here. "Hi Gert" he says into her apartment answering machine, "I must have just missed you.

"I want to let you know I am alive and well. Thanks for the bike. The bike and your steady generosity set off a whole week of good luck which has turned into more good luck. So, wanted to thank you... I am going to get my van back today... I'll see you eh?"

Dave promises to look after the pups tonight if for some reason they get delayed. Jerry's guess is this idea has come straight from Geoffrey. Dave is more of an, in the moment kind of guy. Melvin has no idea that Geoff will be tagging along too and for the first time Melvin does not seem so lighthearted.

When Geoff arrives, he says, "Good to meet you Melvin. Hope you two don't mind but I brought some work to do. I'll just sit in the back and get to it." Geoffrey's good at reading people and as soon as he said that Melvin lightened up. Melvin was a one on one person, who when spinning a tale preferred to do so with an audience of only one.

Slipping on some ear buds with a bit of drama, Geoff lets them know by the action, he will not hear a word they say. It is just after six in the morning by the time they get rolling and Geoff who ate his own body weight each day, is already getting hungry. Tapping Melvin on the shoulder, he interrupts Melvin's monologue long enough to say,

"Hey, can we stop in White Rock or maybe Blaine. I'm starving, I'd like to take you two for something to eat." Ever since Geoff learned to drive on Gran's SUV, he prefers to do the driving. He is a nervous passenger so brought his ear buds to be distracted by music while Melvin was behind the wheel.

Before he starts listening, he overhears a snippet of conversation that makes him smile. Up front Melvin casts a long look at Geoff in the mirror and a side long look at his front seat passenger. "So that's your grandson? He must look like his dad because he sure doesn't look like you."

"Geoff? Sure, he does he has my height, my head of hair and his grandmother's eyes." As soon as the words were out of his mouth, Maeve with her dark eyes sprang to mind. He wondered if he would ever see her again.

Theirs had been a chance meeting the first time he ran into her. Another chance meeting last week outside the Greek Deli; but that time, she missed seeing him until it was too late. And the other time outside the grocery store when he still carried the bruises of his beating.

As soon as she bent at the waist that time to slip the fiver in his hat it was the gesture and the hemline that he recognized. Recognition made him turn his head away in fear of detection. Three times he had seen her out of the blue. So, what are the chances of that?

His wife Jan would say - there are no coincidences Jerry. And she might have added to that – there is a good chance he will see his new friend again. He sure hoped so. Pops was in his own little world and completely misses what Melvin is saying, but he hears Geoff's name.

"Ah sorry Melvin, I didn't quite catch that last bit."

"Oh, it was nothing, just a bit of advice. I said if you are going to give the van to the kid make him put up some money. Then he'll really look after it; you know, he will have a personal stake – am I right? To me he looks like a bit of a nerd, not a car guy at all. Though these days, what do ya call a guy that looks like Geoff? Oh, I know a hipster - am I right? I guess a hipster would like a V Dub; just another throw back, to hippy days."

"Oh, don't worry about that Melvin. Geoff will be paying all right." Jerry had no intention of giving Melvin any impression of him, other than to be a mirror image of Melvin himself, parroting back tit for tat.

IT FEELS like it's been a long drive. Turning in his seat he taps Geoff on the knee. "Hey, son we're at the border better get your passport ready." Once through the border Melvin catches Geoff's attention before he puts his ear buds back in.

"Sorry Buddy, but I don't have time to stop; I'm already behind in my day. There is a good place to eat right next to my garage though. You two can go there, the foods not bad. But I need to see how the guys are doing this morning. Without the boss man around to check their work - you know what they say, when the cats away..."

Geoff's stomach grumbling nods a no problem signal, but Geoff feels like he might vomit if he does not get something in him soon. It is then he feels a long arm snake back toward him. Between the front seat and the door, is Pop's hand holding a wrapped half sandwich; Pops gives it a jiggle.

Grabbing hold and taking a bite Geoff is reminded of his Gran and her habit of always carrying food with her. His hand reaches over top of the seat to pat Pops on the shoulder and never hears what Melvin says, "You spoil him Mr. Landvik." A smiling Pops is glad to save Geoff from hunger. It is a small pay back that is all it is.

BARELY SAYING A WORD, the whole ride Pops is relieved to arrive at the garage and see the back of his van. He almost missed the look of disappointment the guys in the garage had on their faces when they saw the boss man was back a lot earlier than they would have liked.

Pops never waited for either Melvin or Geoff to get out of the car. He went straight for the van. Unlocking the driver's door, he hops in, looking ready to drive away. Then remembering; it is Geoff who will be doing the driving. Stepping back out he goes around the other side opening the double side doors and the passenger door too. They all seem to work fine. Next, he checks the body for scratches and the interior for damage. Absolutely nothing has been touched.

His storage system was left alone and intact. He looks up to see Geoff watching him from the office. Geoff has his credit card out. Melvin takes the card, then leaning forward tells Geoffrey,

"Having a van like that? Will be a lot of work and very pricey. Like when you two get back? It will need some work. Where do you take it?" When Geoff admits he has no idea Melvin is sure the old guy is making a big mistake putting this young guy on title.

"I told your granddad you ought to pay him something to go on title. Don't take advantage of the guy, OK? Even though he's your grandfather; especially because he's your grandfather." If the last comment were heard by Pops it would have caused further irritation. But when Geoff hears it, Melvin endears himself. Pulling a couple of Canadian hundreds out of his jeans pocket he says,

"Don't worry, I'll always treat Pops right. And Melvin thanks for taking the time, really appreciate all you've done. I can see you're backed up here so," Smacking the hundreds on the counter Geoff says "...for your trouble and breakfast is still on me. I need to get Pops home though. He still needs to renew his license and we just might make it before the license place gets too busy."

Melvin walks Geoff out to the garage watching with envy as he climbs into the driver's seat. The motor turns over first try thanks to Melvin getting the guys to put the battery on the charger overnight. When he throws the V Dub into reverse though, the whole van screeches and jerks on its way out of the garage. And the old man looks like he is going to have a heart attack.

Laughing Melvin turns back to his work thinking Geoff and Mr. Landvik were going to butt heads on the way back to Canada. Once on the road the driving smooths out and driving a stick shift comes back to Geoff. He is still hungry and says so. Pops laughs saying, "A young guy like you is always hungry. Stop when you like Geoff and you may treat me to lunch. How much was the tab back there by the way?"

"Don't worry about it Pops. For now at least, but I'll keep a running tab for you and when you're flush you can pay me; or better yet if you ever do want to sell the van, we can take it off the asking price; is that fair?"

"Geoff don't worry I can pay back the money. I just don't know how I can pay back your kindness to me." They drove in silence for a long time after that. Geoff is not used to people thanking him or showing gratitude. He feels his own life at times has been so lacking, that what he does for others now is his way of making up to a little boy, who got lost in the shuffle of disfunction.

Two parents who should not have been parents; his mother a drunken druggie, his father a man with such low self-esteem that for a long time he could not even keep a job. Then his dad fell into being the expert in selling time shares and things got a lot better.

Geoff's one piece of luck was in having his Gran and Stan. Overall, he lived at Gran's about half his life, either full time or weekends and holidays and before and after school.

His Gran could take credit for noticing her grandson was a genius and needed special help in order to shine, as she liked to say.

Once through the border Geoff pulls over to look at his cell phone and find the nearest licensing renewal location. Turning to look at his clearly nervous passenger he says, "Good news Pops, we'll pull into Cloverdale and get your license renewed there. Then you can drive." Smiling broadly, Geoff pulls back into traffic with a satisfied and relieved looking man in the passenger seat, who is still clutching the door for safety.

Once in and out of the comparatively quiet Cloverdale drivers licensing office and Pops was behind the wheel once more. Before starting up the VW Jerry reaches under his front seat touching his finger on a photo album. He pulls it out, passing it over to Geoff with a sense of relief that it is still there.

"This book contains the highlights of some of the trips this van has been on. It has had one rebuilt engine and about five years ago a brand new one. That cost a fortune. Any time work needs to be done, if I cannot do it myself it costs a bundle. So early on I took charge of basic maintenance at least; like oil changes and making sure all the fluids were up. I have never driven it in snow but good tires at a decent price are hard to find.

"Instead of watching Jordan playing at piano recitals, I worked on the van. Instead of going to dinners with Jan to her friends places I took a drive. I guess I was not around much. But that's life Geoff. You cannot live a life to please another person. What joy would there be in that eh? But if I had the chance to do it differently, I would have sold the van."

Had he created a memory of an idyllic world of family

vacations, weekends, and joy rides? It was not real was it. When did he rewrite history, while it happened or after it was all over when his two family members were dead? Driving down the highway glad to be behind the wheel, the insights rolling in are encouraging. Like the big waves along the west coast of Vancouver Island.

His wife read a lot of self-help books. As she read them, she mentioned insights too, but he never wanted to know more. As far as he knew his son never had an insight, until the last days of his illness, when he took his mother's hand and said he liked being with her more than anyone else on earth.

He said he loved the way she anticipated his every need. Holding her hand while he said it, Jerry knew it was true. Lost in thoughts of the past, suddenly they are already back in Vancouver.

Turning his head Pops says, "I'll drop you at Dave's? I've got a date with my gal Maeve and I want to pick up some mail. In fact, I've got to do a bit of running around before I go back to be with Stella and the pups for the night."

Geoff must get back on the job too. He is behind in his work hours and his schoolwork as well. When they arrive in the lane behind the bike shop, Dave steps out to have a look and to show Pops where the van can park temporarily.

"I also found a covered secure place for you to park if you want it. $150 a month but it's on the west side. Up around Dunbar and 20th...is that too far? There's lots of hills in that area; it might be a bit of a climb for you on the bike." Pops has told Dave he has always parked his van undercover. He rarely drives it - just once a week and the rest of the time he walks or catches a bus.

But now that he has a bike, he plans to get around on that. He also told Dave about the little dog he gave away when Dave was almost going to offer him a pup. Second thoughts dictated the pups get placed in stable homes.

Stella hears the familiar sound of Pops voice. Racing out the door into the lane for the handout she can count on Pops for. "If you don't mind Dave, I'm going to park her right now; there are too many crazy drivers around this afternoon." While he backs into his spot, Dave grabs Stella by the collar and Geoff regales Dave with the thrill of driving the van - and driving Pops nuts at the same time.

CHAPTER FIFTEEN

"We stopped off in Cloverdale to get his license renewed. I could not face the number one highway. It was bad enough on highway 15, Pops was hanging on for dear life, with me behind the wheel...

"It's good of you Dave to help him out like this. I owe ya!" With arms crossed over their chests they watch Pops as he takes a small bucket and cloth to begin wiping down the van. Then he takes a chamois to the windows. It looks like a routine done for years. And one that ensures the van is in mint condition just as Melvin had told him it was. Melvin gave a rough estimate of how high a collector would go to get this van. Even half was more than Geoff could afford.

POPS PUTS his leg over the seat of his bike and hears Dave call out, "Hey Pops wait up a sec... I've got something for you." Beaconing for him to follow Dave goes inside to rummage through the contents of a box. Pulling out a pair of cyclists' long pants and a jacket, he motions for Pops to take them.

"Here. These are for you; I'm fairly sure they'll fit you Pops but honestly every time I see you head off, I'm afraid your pants will get caught in the spokes. If you are going to ride around Vancouver, you gotta look the part." Holding the cycling gear out Pops does not budge. As a final argument Dave says,

"I've got to stay working on a few things till about eight tonight. This here jacket has reflective material - in other words - you don't need to rush back for Stella. When you're riding around at night, man, you sure need to be seen."

"Dave you've already done so much for me. I don't know what to say and I can't pay you for any of this?"

"No sweat man. You've been doing lots around here. Don't worry about it. Just take them OK?" Pops burst into laughter. There was no obvious reason. But through a giddy nervous chuckle he said, "Clothes make the man, right?"

Before Pops leaves to change, as afterthought Dave thrusts a thermal riding shirt at him to wear. And next he would do something about the shoes Pops had on.

Pops came back down the stairs looking like a changed man. Dave noticed a fresh shave as well. He truly looked like a cyclist riding off down the lane.

Gert's pet store was in complete darkness. Her back in fifteen minutes sign was not hung in the window. Using his key Jerry opens the street level door that takes him up a set of stairs to the apartment above.

Knocking quietly before using his key, Jerry presses his ear against the door listening for sounds of life. Almost falling in, the door swings open, and there is Gert standing arms akimbo. Dropping them when she sees who it is, she throws both arms around the new man before her.

"Jerry you're back. God dammit. I've been worried sick about you. Got your message this morning... don't just stand there come in." Jerry edges past Gert who partially blocks the doorway. Gert is not taken in by Jerry's outer look of good fortunes. "Who gave you the new duds? You look good Jerry. You look like a cyclist. The bike, I trust is working out?"

Heading for the kitchen and a glass of water; Jerry leans up against the counter. He fills Gert in on all the good stuff that has been happening. Beginning with the gift of the bike. "You are a generous person Gert; you know I can never repay you - don't you?"

"Well I didn't want to say it in the note and if you couldn't see it for yourself... that bike is or was, Jordan's bike. And the helmet, baskets, panniers too... Eric brought them by."

Pops instant reaction is anger at Eric followed in a tick by love for Jordan. In his mind's eye he can see his son riding low over the handlebars. And yes - on this bike with all its appendages. Jerry had not even recognized it as his son's.

Gert's saying so brings a flood of memories rushing back. Jordan and his bike and cycling were all important to Jordan. As important as the van is to Jerry. This is the first time Jerry ever feels his son resembles him in any way - for the love of the wheels.

Jerry knows his bikes were Jordan's prized possessions and now this one is his. Unsure of the reaction she would get when he found out, Gert's thrilled the news she delivered is well received.

"One more thing Jerry, before I forget... You know the woman you introduced me to? Maeve? She keeps calling here looking for you and says to give you her number the minute you come in." Spinning around flicking on Gert's computer - Jerry asks for the number. While he waits, he sets the computer up at the reverse directory site hoping he can find Maeve's address. If so, he plans to make a surprise visit.

Jerry sticks around long enough for Gert to blow her top when she discovers when Jerry arrived no one was in the shop below and there was no – back in fifteen minutes sign either. Melisa was AWOL again it seemed.

What Gert hoped would be a restful afternoon of lying about in the apartment, finishing her novel, and catching up on some sleep evaporated. Though Jerry's offer to do duty in the store for a couple of hours, gives Gert a good feeling; she sends Jerry on his way to see Maeve.

JACK GOES CRAZY. His sharp barking and scratching at the door make Mavis think there is a squirrel or some other rodent outside tormenting her little pal. When she goes to peek out the window, she sees not a thing. The small yard is empty of man or beast; but Jack persists.

Mavis cannot see into the lane unless she goes upstairs to look out a window. So that is what she does. And Jack follows close behind. No sooner does she open the window for a better view, Jack is turning circles in the upstairs hall barking. Racing down the stairs - this time he sounds frantic from his spot in front of the door.

The late afternoon sun is almost gone, and Mavis feels unsettled with the mad barking, but she heads into the kitchen when she hears someone knocking, over all the barking. Right before her eyes, there stands Jerry.

The man she could not get out of her mind is on her

little deck, a bike helmet in hand; waiting for his little lady to open the door. Pushing up the latch on her glass door Mavis gets it open and Jack's outside jumping and barking. Both adults lean over the dog to calm him and come face to face.

Feeling a slight brush of freshly shaved cheek against hers is the first she has felt in years. A thrill of something unidentifiable, shudders up her spine, leaving her breathless. Jerry takes her hands in his, lifting them both up and away from the dog. They face each other. Jerry says, "Hello Maeve; I've sure missed you."

"Come in." Is all she can think to reply; she never let go his hand though. She draws him into the living room where they both collapse on the sectional in a laughing heap with a barking happy dog on top.

CHARLENE'S CHOMPING at the bit to get out of the house and over to her Gran's place. Her mother will not take her there and does not want her riding the bus all the way there on her own. It is Thursday. There is no school tomorrow because of a Professional Development day for the teachers. Charlene had forgotten so did not tell Geoffrey she could go a day early.

She wished she had asked Geoffrey for a ride today instead of tomorrow. Doreen's in the house yelling at the boys to clean their rooms as if anyone would set foot in them on Sunday during the memorial for Robin. Charlene imagines it will only be family here to send her grandfather off anyway. He was a dink with a capital D. If only her mother knew the sort of stunt he tried to pull every time he could. When he had legs that is.

One time, at a New Year's Eve party Doreen had thrown, Charlene saw his hand snaking around a crowd of revellers to grab the butt of Ricki. Doreen would put up with shit like that, but not Ricki.

When she saw who it was, she stood in front of him and reached between his legs. From what his grinning gob inferred, he thought there was going to be an invitational grope. Ricki squeezed him fast and hard.

Granddad let out a yelp and staggered, doubled over into the washroom. After that Ricki invited all the kids including Charlene, to her place. Charlene loved going to Ricki's place. It was clean and always warm when she went there, even if she just dropped in. Ricki usually had a home-made snack ready to share or would make peanut butter and jam on toast, with tea.

The school day was at an end and Doreen was meant to have Ricki's kids today because her other childcare fell through for this week. They were supposed to come straight here from school. Doreen is sitting at the kitchen table shouting out orders to the boys when Charlene arrives home. She is drinking too, right next to a growing stack of empties. Some parents would have the smarts to conceal their booze in a coffee cup, not Doreen.

She takes one of the good fancy glasses with ice and all, like a party. Charlene stands perfectly still outside the door wondering how long it will take for her mother to notice her. If she does not move until Doreen leaves the kitchen; she might be able to get away before her mother sees her. Too late though Charlene sees those drunken blue eyes shift her way. Then bang goes the glass on the tabletop. Doreen bellows.

"Get in here!" The whole neighbourhood will hear. Cringing, Charlene tries to slide the door open, but it is locked. Shrieking for one of the twins to come open it up, Doreen looks furious and Charlene wants to be anywhere else. Both twins come running into the kitchen and open the slider on its broken wheel making a loud scraping sound.

Thanking the boys nicely, Doreen pushes back from the table and says, "Did you hear that door screech? You never contacted maintenance about that Frigg 'in door - did ya?" Charlene protests, saying she told the site manager on her way to school, "She told me if we could still open the door it wasn't an emergency. She said she has got to make a work order up mum. I did do it."

"You F'ing little liar. I phoned over there myself an hour ago and no one knew anything. You're grounded Charlene; go to your room; just get out of my sight you ugly pig."

"You can't ground me; I'm going to Gran's tomorrow to help her cook... for granddad's party."

"You are not going to see Mavis. And help her cook? What a laugh, are you kidding me? You can't cook. If you could don't you think I would have noticed? You never asked me if you could go Charlene, and you ain't going anywhere. Period! Get to your room. Now!"

Tears spill from Charlene's eyes as she trips up the stairs. The twins at the top are snickering because they heard the whole thing. For some reason Butch and Robby never got a smack or any real grief from their mother. Charlene bets they will the minute they start to contradict her.

Pushing past the boys to her room she is greeted by a mess. Someone has been in here looking for something. The whole room has been tossed and looks like the result of a robbery. Closing and latching her door behind her, she goes to the closet. Her little pink box is gone. That's where her babysitting money from Ricki is kept. Safe in the pink box.

Storming back down the stairs Charlene pushes past the boys, toppling one of them halfway down the staircase. Charlene marches indignantly into the kitchen. In a calm calculated voice, she says, "You took my money."

Doreen in the same spot at the table, with fresh drink in hand, slides her rummy eyes to stare a smirk at Charlene, "Of course I took your money doll. Didn't I tell ya? I want room and board now." Charlene did not expect that; what she really wants is the little pink leatherette box the money had been tucked inside.

"Where's the box Doreen."

"You - don't call me Doreen! You! Do not ever call me Doreen, god dammit! You know I hate that!" Doreen is outraged. "I don't know where your stupid pink box is. It's probably in the dumpster by now, you stupid twit."

Charlene burst into tears. Her father gave her the box last time she saw him; she was seven. He came to pick her up for the weekend. An arrangement had been made for a visit but only after her dad had jumped through the hoops of Doreen's rules.

Doreen always insisted he run his minute by minute plans by her for approval and then would leave him hanging for long as possible before saying yes...or too often it would be - no. She did the same with Charlene's paternal grandparents who had doted on her. When her dad arrived ten minutes early, Doreen had one of her screaming fits. At the last minute she said Charlene could not go with him.

Doreen picked up Charlene's pink music box, tore out the tiny pink ballet dancer and smashed the mirror in the lid. Doreen told Charlene's dad he was not going to be allowed to take Charlene anywhere ever again on his own.

She told him, from now on he would need supervised visits. And no more overnight visits ever.

The seven-year-old Charlene stood quietly on the same stairs she had just come down and watched as her dad looked broken. He picked up the damaged box. Taking Charlene's hand, they both went into the basement where he reconfigured her music box with a cardboard sign inside the lid where the mirror had been.

In his handwriting it said - Smile and you will always be beautiful to those who know you. When it was all done, they left by the basement door and went to the cafe on the corner. He told Charlene; it would be better if she did not see him for a while. It was better for her, better for her mother and better for him too.

He brought her home and said goodbye. She never heard from him for a long time until one day he wrote her from his new home in Edmonton. It was Geoffrey who taught her how to write a letter back. Then when she was eleven it was Geoffrey who set her up with email so she could stay in touch with him that way.

Her Gran said, "Sometimes when good loyal people are pushed away too hard and too many times, they just give up, and save what's left of themselves. I think that's what happened Charlene. Do not hold it against him, OK sweetie? He stays connected in a way that he's comfortable with. And when you get older you can visit him in Edmonton."

Until right this minute Charlene never knew what Gran had meant. But her mother had just thrown out the most precious belonging Charlene had. She now knew what it felt like to be pushed around. Her mother had gone too far. Back up the stairs Charlene went. This time with resolve.

Her little brothers did not look so chuffed this time, they

looked scared. Neither had ever been allowed to touch or look at Charlene's music box. Following her to her room they watched as she began sorting through her things, stuffing selected items into a much-used backpack.

Whispering Butch grabbed Charlene's sleeve and asked his older sister, "Are you running away Charlene? With a finger to her lips, Charlene told them, "Don't ask; don't tell." Both boys knew what that meant. The less they knew the better and told her they had not seen a thing.

Backing out of her door they return to their post at the top of the stairs to watch and listen. Once Charlene is packed, she whispers to the boys to go in the kitchen and keep Doreen busy while she exits through the front door without Doreen hearing.

But Doreen hears all right and she is at the front door pressing her wide hips against it faster than Charlene can get there. Throwing a chair down to block her mothers' path, Charlene makes a quick turn into the kitchen, managing to get out the stuck sliding glass door a hair ahead of Doreen.

Without shoes on Doreen hangs screaming in the door-way. She calls after Charlene all the way down the parking lot; and keeps right on yelling when Charlene disappears around the corner. It will be dark in another hour. By that time Doreen will be dead drunk and passed out until morning.

Geoffrey tries Charlene on her cell before driving all the way to Surrey on Friday. He is hoping he can get her to come in on the SkyTrain and meet him halfway. But the last time he suggested that Charlene got grounded for asking Doreen if it would be OK. Doreen chastised Geoffrey over the phone saying there were perverts on that train and Charlene would not be going on it without an adult.

As far as Geoffrey knew Charlene had never caught the sky train by herself. Not that she was molly coddled it was just that she was in walking distance to school and Doreen kept her on a very tight leash. Not for the first time, Geoffrey viewed his mother's parenting skills as contradictory.

When he got to the house it was about four in the afternoon. The twins were outside throwing rocks at a kitten that was backed up into the corner of a fence. Geoffrey got hold of the collar of the twin closest and gave him a shake.

"What the heck do you think you're doing?" Geoffrey dropped him like a hot potato when the kid squealed like an injured animal; felt guilty, fearing he was just like his mother. "Sorry Rob but hurting kittens - just is not cool man."

"But mum told us to do it. She said to make sure it never came back in the yard, Geoffrey."

"That's not how you do it, my man." Geoffrey now trying to act friendly and cool to regain the twins' trust. He never warmed to the twins but mainly because he could not stand their dad Keith which was not their fault.

Geoffrey wished he were a better brother and a better person. He would like to be a good role model for them but doubted he would be able to step up to the plate when Doreen wouldn't even let them alone with him - if she could help it. Right now, though, it was freezing cold outside.

"Come on, I'll follow you into the house. Is Charlene home from school yet?" The twins exchanged a nervous look before telling Geoffrey, there was no school today "Pro D Day."

"OK, well is she in the house then?" Again, the nervous

look between brothers but this time Geoffrey caught it and asked what was up. The whole story came out. The argument between mother and daughter; Charlene had packed a backpack. And their mother had gone to sleep after that.

They had to make dinner for themselves because their dad had not come home either and told them he wasn't ever coming back. Before Geoffrey stepped into the house to find out what the heck was going on Butch pulled him back.

"Please don't tell mum we saw Charlene with the backpack. She ran away."

"When was this again guys?"

"After School."

"Yesterday?" Geoffrey asked just to get it straight. The boys resisted going back in the house telling Geoffrey their mum, Doreen was in a bad mood because she was sick. She told them to go play. Just then Geoffrey sees Ricki looking at them from her kitchen window. He waves, and she opens her door a crack.

"Hey, Ricki, can the boys come in for a little while? And you wouldn't know where Charlene is would you?"

"Yes, they can come in and no I don't know where Charlene is; your mum already asked me. Come on in guys. I'll make something to warm you up...hot chocolate; you'd like that wouldn't ya? But Geoffrey I'm taking my kids out in about an hour, so I'll send the boys home before that - OK?"

Giving Ricki a nod and thumbs up, Geoffrey goes to the back door of his mother's place. She is holding court at an empty table. She has a drink in one of her finest glasses and looks like she has been crying. Geoffrey taps on the glass then yanks the sliding door open. Knowing the best way to approach Doreen so that he gets the information he wants, is to be calm and friendly. He steps over to the sink and pours himself some water then sits down at the table.

"Are you OK Mum? You must be pretty upset about your dad; did you get the flowers?" She had gotten the flowers from Geoffrey and his girlfriend and tossed them out in a huff. They arrived at a tough time; she was upset. But when wasn't she upset these days?

Ever since Mavis stopped coming, things were going downhill fast around here. Something Doreen was not willing to admit though. She didn't want to admit she had thrown the flowers out either, so she told a lie.

"I didn't get them Geoffrey but thanks for thinking of me." Geoffrey felt an instant anger because he knew she was lying. The tell was her pleasantness. If she really had not gotten the flowers, she would be indignant. Geoffrey internally calmed himself.

"I've come to get Charlene but before we leave how about Charlene and I make some dinner for you and the boys?"

"Oh No Geoffrey. Charlene is grounded so she can't go with you. And that's that." Still playing it cool Geoffrey says that's OK but still he wants to make sure the boys and his mum eat and Charlene too, before he leaves. All he wants is for her to say Charlene is gone. She doesn't. Getting up from the table Geoffrey sticks his head around the corner and shouts up the stairs for Charlene.

"She's not there Geoffrey she went out."

"I thought you said she was grounded?"

"She is grounded but you know what she's like. She didn't listen. She went out."

"When?"

"After school I guess."

"You mean after school today?" Hesitating Doreen toys with the idea of lying to Geoffrey, instead she comes out with it. "No. Yesterday! She got mad about something and

181

just stormed out of here. I thought she would be back, but the twins said no. She didn't come home - the little slag."

"Have you called the police?"

"The police? Are you kidding what would they do? Teenagers run away all the time. You know that. You even ran away once. Do you remember?"

"Yeah..." says Geoffrey digging his phone out of his pocket. Dialling his grandmother, he asks if she has seen Charlene or heard from her. Doreen only hears one side of the conversation and what she hears makes her stomach turn. How Geoffrey can talk about her like this she wonders and finally she says, "I'm right here Geoffrey.

"Right here! Have some respect!" Covering the phone so his Gran doesn't hear he says, "That's rich coming from you. I need all Charlene's friend's numbers Doreen; right now. Write them down for me while I finish with Gran."

Geoffrey went in the other room and told Gran not to worry yet that she would be OK. He would call the police to file a missing person's report and call to let her know, if he hears anything.

"Do you think she would try to come here Geoffrey? Do you think she even knows how to get here?" And that's the big question Geoffrey has on his mind too. He knows his sister and knows if she had the money and knew how, she would get the bus to Gran's. "Geoffrey my friend is here now so I'll put a note for Charlene on the door and we'll go out around the neighbourhood and see if she's wandering around somewhere. If she calls the voice mail will pick up.

"I know what I'll do – I'll record a special message letting her know I'm here to welcome her with open arms." They promised to stay in touch and agreed to talk in an hour.

CHAPTER SIXTEEN

W hen Mavis turns after she hangs up the phone, she looks to Jerry as if she has seen the proverbial ghost. All the colour had left her face. Even her dark eyes look void of the usual light. Standing with a blank look on her face she suddenly turns to take a couple of pictures off the side of the fridge and hands one to Jerry.

"This is my granddaughter, Charlene. You heard me just now; I was talking to my grandson. She is missing; maybe she's on her way here; we just don't know. All I know is she left yesterday at this time from Surrey. Jerry do you think you can ride your bike safely down to the sky train station and show her picture around for me? Please? I just don't know what else to do.

"I'll take Jack just around here down to Broadway and ask in the Greek Deli she might remember we went there once long ago. The police have been called and they are on their way to my daughter's house to take information."

Mavis wasn't finished talking and Jerry was already slipping into the new cycling jacket with reflective strips that Dave gave him yesterday afternoon. Taking the picture, he headed out the door. He knows it was a long shot looking for a lost kid he's never met. But he's happy to do it for his little lady.

This morning had seemed like a lifetime ago. Yesterday afternoon's reunion had turned into an afternoon of delight that surprised them both. The two had a long bath together afterwards, washing each other from head to toe. A long sleep followed a bit of supper and then it was time for Jerry to get back on his bike and back to Stella.

But first thing in the morning as soon as Dave turned up Jerry was back on the road to see his gal. And that's what he told Dave, saying he would be back later, after dinner. Maeve was sitting sipping coffee with a dreamy look in her eye when he returned first thing and they had been alone together all day.

They talked about the past and about their marriages. Jerry talked about Jordan. And Maeve listened. By the end of the day Maeve had asked Jerry an important question and he had said yes. Reluctantly he was getting ready to go back to Stella, when Geoffrey called to say Charlene was missing,

RIDING down Broadway is going to be quicker than stepping on a bus so that's what Jerry does. Weaving in and out of traffic feels natural as if he were born to ride. He covers the distance in record time. The sky train platform crawls with people. The first ones he talks to are security and then he talks to homeless people outside the station. He shows Charlene's picture over and over and then he decides he will hop on a train and ride to Surrey.

He locks his bike and buys a ticket to ride. When the

train draws alongside him, he sees her. She is disembarking from the train that had come in the opposite direction. "Charlene." He shouts. "Over here."

The girl on the opposite platform turns to look at him. She begins moving with some speed, away and further down the platform. Keeping watch over her shoulder making sure he doesn't follow. But he does and over the roar of the train shouts over and over, "Your grandmother sent me."

Charlene's scared; she's spent the last twenty-four hours catching buses going up and down Broadway back and forth to Surrey. Cell reception on the train was bad then she lost her charge all together. She ran out of money for the train the night before but ended up in Surrey. She walked to her best friend Dorothy's place.

Dorothy had a basement apartment that she lived in on her own. Her landlord said no friends overnight, or past ten. The girls had to be super quiet. When Dorothy got a call at about 11:30PM she made a date to go stay over with her new boyfriend, Alex.

Promising Charlene, she would be back first thing in the morning Dorothy headed off. Dorothy didn't come home first thing and the next thing Charlene knew the landlord spotted her through Dorothy's kitchen window and told her to get out.

Before she went, she borrowed some lose change on the table and Dorothy's monthly bus pass hanging from her door handle; then skedaddled. Walking all the way back to the sky train station, Charlene soon found herself riding back and forth again.

She knew she could not do it forever. As soon as she got the courage, she planned to panhandle for some money for the pay phone and call for help. Her mum had been right about Vancouver; there were a lot of weirdo's.

Right across the platform one guy in a cyclist suit was waving and shouting at her. Hurrying down the platform Charlene is disorientated and knows she needs help. She keeps looking over her shoulder to watch for the man stalking her. So, intent on making sure he isn't behind her, lurking in shadows she did not notice the cyclist standing at the bottom of the steps.

She never panicked when she saw him right in front of her waiting. A calm of resignation came over her. It felt like what happened inside her when her mother was on a rant and no way to escape it.

"Charlene!" She stopped dead, turning toward the voice and before she could run the other way Jerry reached out and put his hand around her wrist and said in a slow firm voice, "Your grandmother, sent me to find you. You're Charlene, aren't you? Is this your picture?" Out of his pocket came Charlene's high school picture. With relief, she suddenly felt safety with white haired man. Charlene began to cry.

So, trusting of this stranger she found herself pressing her head into his shoulder with complete relief that someone was there to help. The two stood like that for minutes as people incuriously passed them by. Taking her hand Jerry introduced himself and said he could not take her on his bike, "Your Grandmother said to send you in a taxi."

Escorting her across the street, Jerry got her safely in a cab headed to her grandmother's, where a bowl of soup would be waiting. Then he called Maeve. Charlene, he said, is fine. A bit tired and shaken up but fine. Asked if she could stay the night with her Gran and said she didn't want her mother to come over or even Geoffrey. "She just wants you my sweet Maeve. Shall I see you tomorrow morning, love?"

Love. He called her love. They had each expressed their love. She told him first. "I loved you the moment I saw you. It was before I heard you shouting at Jack. Jack Off, Jack Off - it made me laugh inside. But first when I saw you two standing side by side - I loved you."

Jerry's words of love followed hers with each of them feeling confidant their love was the real thing. "Soul mates..." Jerry dared to say as he cradled her tidy body in a hairy embrace. He loved her and with great relief that he had found her again.

"Yes please. Come tomorrow. We'll take Jack for a walk together first and then have breakfast with Charlene. She'll want to sleep late so we will have time on our own. I love you Jer. Thank you, thank you... Will you call me before you go to bed?" Smiling Jerry nodded into the phone. Slinging his leg over the seat of his bike he peddled off in the direction of the bike shop.

WHEN HE GOT THERE, it was long after dark and Dave's almost given up on seeing Pops again that day. Jerry taps his knuckles on the back door before opening it up. Dave is sitting on the steps in his own bike gear; Stella by his side with her head on his lap, gazing up at his face. Dave and Stella both jump when they see Pops. He looks like a new man, self-assured. Stella wiggles next to him nuzzling his pocket looking for a treat before he even gets his bike put away. "Glad you got here before I left Pops. I was just about to leave you a note."

"What's up, everything OK Dave?" Pops casts concerned

eyes toward waiting Stella and then upstairs. Dave sees where his concern lay and feels assured again that Pops was the right guy to look after the pups. "No. Everything is fine here.

"Geoff just called to let you know not to expect him tonight; he has a family emergency." There was something else Dave wanted to tell Pops, but he wasn't sure about the details. Almost leaving it for another day.

"Oh, and Pops, I have good news and bad news and other good news too I suppose. The good news is my girl-friend, and I will be moving into the upstairs apartment in the house she rents. Somehow, she talked the owner into allowing a dog. So, this is, including Stella...and the pups. She managed to do this partly because the main floor tenants took off after not paying rent for a couple of months. They left the place in a big mess.

"The bad news is I won't need you after the weekend to look after Stella not here at least." Holding up his hand for silence, he continued, "You can stay upstairs for as long as it takes to get it together Pops. Then you can either pay rent or find another place."

"OK. Well thanks for letting me know. Sorry Stella, we won't be seeing much of each other. I knew it wasn't anything permanent Dave, so don't feel bad about it. I'm glad for you - and for Stella she misses you at night."

"I might need you to swing by to the new place though Pops. I can't take time off to go check on Stella and the pups during the day. She'll be in a strange place and I was wondering if you can do that for me. I'll pay you of course."

Pops laughed at that and slapping Dave on the back made his way upstairs to see the pups and give his gal a call. Before he left her tonight to look for Charlene Maeve had slipped her cell phone and charger into a side pocket of his coat and told him to use it when he got back here.

WHEN CHARLENE GOT out of the taxi her Gran is waiting on the street to pay the cab driver and get her granddaughter inside. Shivering, Charlene forgets all her own worries when they enter Gran's place and Jack makes his presence known. "Who's this Gran? I love him." Sliding down to sit on the floor Charlene and Jack get to know each other while Mavis turns the soup pot back on.

"That's Jack. Jerry gave him to me; my friend that met you at the sky train? Jack is his dog really; well I guess, he is our dog." Mavis put hand to heart as she said these last words realizing he was their dog.

Finally, they sit across the table from each other. Charlene and Mavis are completely focused on the little dog as he sits on his mat waiting for his turn at a bit of soup. Both are quiet. Mavis waits for Charlene to tell her what happened; Charlene is content to not be pressed to have to tell what happened. She is grateful not to be grilled like she would be at home.

She feels a calm settling over her; one that she never once has felt under the microscope of her mother, the inquisitor. Just as Gran began to suggest a nice long bath after dinner the phone rings. Stumbling out of her chair with a grin on her face Mavis answers before the second ring. "Jer hi...yes we just sat down to eat. You made it home fast." followed by silence.

Charlene had become adept at knowing all by listening to one sided conversation. But this time she knew it all by the expression on her Grandmother's face. Charlene had never known her Gran to be happy and exuberant. She wasn't a misery; it wasn't that at all. She was matter of fact.

And if truth be told when around Doreen, Mavis was careful not to tip the apples out of the cart. This was advice she once shared with Charlene. "Don't argue with your mother, don't talk, just listen Charlene and you won't upset the apple cart."

Right now, it was her grandmother who was listening. Charlene watched while she held the phone pressed tightly to her ear. Her grandmother's face colour goes from red to pink and back to red again. All the way up her throat, the colour surging like a rising tide. Charlene and Jack both watch an animated Mavis smoothing her hair or hugging her body and stroking her own shoulder like a lover would.

Just before she hangs up Charlene hears a long shuddering sigh and a wistful, "Me too...good night." Before Charlene can ask about the phone call Mavis turns to her granddaughter, takes her face between her two palms and says the most personal and intimate thing to her that anyone ever has.

"Have you ever had your chest fill up with the joy of love Charlene? For a puppy, or for a dog like little Jackie here, or a kitten; or a boy at school...has your chest ever gotten a warm glow inside?

"It feels like it's in your lungs then you feel the whole chest cavity begin to expand with warmth. You know what I mean? I feel my chest filling right up until I feel the thrill of it just spilling right out of my chest. Then onto my lips and into the world that's surrounding me...do you know what I mean?

"I haven't ever felt that Charlene. This is the first time I've felt it. I feel it with Jerry, the man who found you tonight. Especially with Jerry I feel it, but with Jack too. I am turning sixty soon and this is the first time in my life I've felt this way.

"Hold out for love Charlene. Always hold out for the burst of love; then take it slow. Drag the moment out until you think you'll burst. And then you will - over and over." Clasping Charlene's head to her chest Mavis tells her granddaughter, "I am full of love and when you're full of love it spills out for everyone.

"I even love your mother at this moment. But more important, I especially love you. There is nothing you have done or will do that will alter how I feel about you. Good or bad - you can count on my love being steadfast and true.

"I want you to know this Charlene. I will always be here for you; as long as I live." In her Gran's tight hold Charlene let go of a lifetime of angst; a breath out and tears began to flow; dribbling down her face. Tears soaking her Grandmother's blouse and offering a different warmth to both.

Mavis takes Charlene by the hand and guides her upstairs. While she waits for Charlene to arrive in the taxi, Mavis has put clean sheets on her bed. But right now, before she lets Charlene slip between those sheets and into a deep contented sleep, she runs a deep bath with bubbles. Pulling her sweater over her head Mavis helps Charlene undress. Getting out a fresh long white batten-burg lace cotton nighty for sleep, she leaves Charlene to soak.

Then she goes down the stairs to call Doreen. Doreen who has call display calling out the number of who is calling often screens her calls without even looking at the phone. When she hears it is Mavis calling nine times out of ten, she never picks up.

Tonight of course Doreen is sitting right beside the phone and picks it up on the first ring thinking it will be the police. As soon as she hears Mavis, Doreen screams into the phone, "Why are you phoning me? I've gotta keep the line open for the police and Geoffrey! Geoffrey will phone you if we hear any news." With that she hangs up with a bang. Mavis doesn't have time to say a word.

Not being detoured Mavis calls Geoffrey and tells him her friend has gone down to the sky train with a photo and found Charlene. She also tells him, "Charlene wants to stay the weekend and asked if she can come back here next week on the sky train on her own after school Friday.

"I said yes Geoffrey. I want you to sort it out with your mother. She just hung up on me. I called to tell her Charlene was here and she would not even wait to listen to what I had to say. She assumed I knew nothing and hung right up.

"Oh, and another thing you'll have to tell Doreen. Charlene has asked that Doreen not come here. You can pick us both up here on Sunday when we bring the food for Robin's do. But Geoffrey I want you to know, I won't be staying for that.

"I have other plans for the day." They talked on for a while, but Geoffrey was stunned by how light and breezy and confident his Grandmother sounded and he supposed it was the excitement of having found Charlene.

Geoffrey promised to call Doreen and give her all the details and let her know Charlene would be back but not before Sunday. Before she hung up, she asked Geoffrey not to stop by either, "I'd just like some time with Charlene we are never alone just the two of us. I promised to teach her how to cook..."

Not five minutes passed and Doreen calls wanting to speak with Charlene. "You have to let me speak to her. I am her mother. And why didn't you say she was there when you called me. What are you, some kind of idiot? Didn't you think I would want to know?"

"Stop right there Doreen. I have a few things to say and I suggest you listen very carefully. I left your house the last time, never to return because of the way you speak to me on a regular basis. If you think you are going to keep people around by treating them like dirt, you are wrong." Doreen was incensed and tried to interrupt but Mavis just kept right on talking.

"Quit drinking Doreen. You are a drunk. Just like your father... an ugly, ugly drunk. And I am on the other end of the phone, so I feel safe to say that. Do not – ever - let me hear that you have spoken to any of your kids the way you speak to me - Exactly like Robin spoke to me or I will take them from you. I promise you that." Big sobbing sounds were heard on the other end of the line.

"I am going to hang up now Doreen. I am your mother and I find it hard to love you. But I do. So, consider this long overdue tough love, Doreen. Good night." Mavis's heart beats like the wings of an eagle against the walls of her chest. Taking big breaths, she seeks the eyes of her little dog Jack. He has a way of soothing her like none other; but Jack is nowhere to be seen. He is curled up on the bathmat, next to someone who needs him more right now.

Mavis carries sheets and blankets down the stairs, to put on the sectional. Charlene has taken her bed tonight. Mavis wants to be the first-person Jerry sees when he comes through the door the next day.

JERRY'S BEEN busy making a bouquet of branches some with white berries some covered in lichen. When he sees the end of a large sash, hanging out the side of a dumpster he got an inspiration. Following its end, he found the clear cellophane that had once held a bouquet. Taking both back to leave at the shop, he goes outside again to score the flora and fauna lining the boulevards along the main street.

Before he drives the van to the other side of town Pops takes out his best leather jacket, a pair of dress jeans he outgrew ten years ago but seemed to have shrunk back into. And a brand-new purple T-shirt his son had given him long ago. Going upstairs to fetch Stella for one more walk he looks in the mirror; a new man looks back. Not the man he had been - a better man – a man on his way back into the world.

Arriving at his destination he is so taken up again with his reflection in the window of the little house; Jerry doesn't see Maeve right away. It is Jack barking that brings him back to reality. Opening the door for him Maeve says, "You were so deep in thought. No second thoughts about us I hope."

"Oh no, my love, not second thoughts about you. I was just caught up in my own reflection." Jerry picks up and swings Maeve in an arc with barking dog going wild trying to catch her feet while they swing through the air. "Well what was it you saw?" Maeve asks.

Taking just a moment to set her down Jerry places his hands alongside her head, smoothing her hair.

"What I saw in the window my lovely Maeve, was Jerry Resurrected. That's all!" Picking the bouquet up where he cast it, he bows low to say, "For you - the love of my life."

"Oh Jer, they are lovely, and do you know the colour of this sash is so beautiful wherever did you find it? Thank you." Leaning in for a kiss they hear footsteps coming their way. Jerry moves to pull apart, but Maeve holds tight to his hands.

CHARLENE'S REACTION to the sight of her Gran with a man is to grin. Maeve grins back and says, "This man Charlene? He is the love of my life."

Looking from one to the other Charlene smoothly steps forward wraps her arms around her grandmother and around the man who saved her the night before. Pulling back to look at her Gran Charlene asks, "Am I the only one who knows about this Gran?"

Catching Jerry's eyes, Mavis nods her head, "Yes my dear. And for now, it'll be our little secret - OK?" Charlene loves the idea of being the first in on something so big and is glad to keep it to herself for her own special reasons.

CHAPTER SEVENTEEN

Charlene and Mavis work side by side all day preparing a luncheon for Robin's memorial. Mavis makes sure all the bases are covered, with each of her family's favourite dishes represented. She even brought out the recipe for Robin's favourite dessert of apple crisp.

They would have Geoffrey stop on route to pick up ice cream. Mavis said to Charlene as they went about the preparations "When everything gets taken inside, set the oven to about 170 degrees so things can be warm but not hot. I'll make a list of instructions for you pet. Shall I - or will you remember it all; I usually have a check list up for myself.

"But I carry the list around in my head these days. Tell you what; here's paper and pen. You can write down your own check list ok? Oh, and before I forget; I won't be joining you at Doreen's.

"I might not even go for the drive over. Geoffrey and you can handle setting everything up. This is a do for your mother and aunt and for you kids too. There might be some of Robin's old friends there. But I won't be."

"But why not Gran? You've made all the food!"

"We - are making the food. But seriously Charlene if you've noticed anything, it's you who are doing most of the work. You have made the food all on your own Charlene." Charlene drops what she's doing to hug her Gran. Jerry had already left so he didn't see this exchange.

He didn't stay long at all this morning, sensing it was meant to be a girl's day. One he suspected was a long time in the coming. Charlene told him over breakfast this was her first time here and the first time she didn't have to share her Gran with her brother, Geoffrey.

As soon as he heard the name Jerry felt badly that he had not talked to his young friend yet and decided when he got back to the shop; he would give him a call. Or get Dave to. There was something Jerry wanted to ask him.

Saying goodbye was the hardest thing for Jerry; he wanted to stay and be able to prop himself in the little kitchen alcove with the window seat. Reading a paper and watching the two cooks. This was a type of domestication he never experienced with his wife Jan.

With Jan food was quickly prepared. It was last minute meals when she cooked and eating out or take away to bring home. On a Friday and Saturday Jan was off with her friends either at craft fairs or jewellery making workshops. Jerry took a lot of pride in all Jan did and admired how busy she was and how full her life seemed to be.

Even after their son died, she still managed to take courses; not with her friends any longer; all by herself. Neither of them cared for the constant chatter of people with children or grandchildren. Of which they had none to be close to and show off.

And here Jerry was with an opportunity to have a life mate and another chance at a good life once more. To have kids around again and to have a second chance to be better at partnership than he was first go around. Jerry had quietly watched as his little lady glided around her small kitchen. She, in her element, offering a taste of this or that. It was such a temptation to just hang around here all day, but he would go back to Stella and attend to a few jobs on the van.

WHEN HE GOT BACK to Dave's he put on some work clothes and called Geoff from the shop phone. No answer of course so he left a voice message saying he would be at Dave's until five. "There's something I need Geoff. Can you stop by for a while so we can talk?" Handing the cell phone back to Dave Pops headed over to his van with a bucket and a rag. Dave was amazed at how clean he kept the van.

Any concerns he had had about Pops keeping his van there were gone. Not only did Pops keep his van clean, but he also kept the whole shop clean. Dave barely recognized the place when he unlocked each morning. Pops never mentioned whether he would take the garage Dave had found for him or not. He suspected Pops had an idea of his own. Or else he had no money for the garage rental; that was the most likely. He could hear the shop vac going in the van.

Dave walked over, peers in and says, "You sure take care of this van Pops." Feeling a presence at his shoulder, the vacuum turns off and Pops asks if Dave would give him a hand with a few things. They spend the next twenty minutes removing the custom-made bedding platform in the back. Without it, the van is almost empty.

Pops needs to get over to the Bergen house today and make sure all his original seats and everything else from the van are still in the back of the garage. And fingers crossed they are still safely stored so he can re-install them. The van would be back into original condition.

Looking up at the wall clock, Pops puts his hand on Dave's shoulder and says, "I'm going to make us both an early lunch right now then I'll be heading out for a couple of hours. But I really need to talk to Geoff today. And Dave if he calls, tell him I'm selling the van. I'm going to give him first crack...with a catch." Dave was so surprised he could not speak.

This was the last move he expected the old man to make. Worrying that he needed money so badly because he wanted the van under cover, Dave told him he could keep the van here for as long as he liked. Smiling, Pops shakes his head, "Nope.

"You're a good guy Dave and thanks for the offer, but I need the money. I need a bunch of money fast. And I also need to get this van valued by a pro. Got any ideas?" Over lunch Dave cruised around the Internet trying to find a VW club or a specialist. Finally, he picked up the phone and called a European car lot on the west side. Covering the phone with his hand he said to Pops, "Can you take it in today, at about 4:30?" Pops nods yes and springs out of his chair like he has a fire under him.

"I got to get going Dave if I want to make the appointment. Thanks for everything eh?"

"No problem Pops - I didn't do anything. See you later and if you need a hand with the seats bring them back and we can get them in together."

THE LANEWAY GARAGE at Mrs. J's and all its contents are being prepared to be dumped when he gets there. He hops out of the van, running forward with his right hand held straight up in the air. Like a salute. "Stop!" He shouts. He sees two young guys going through the open side door into the building where he had once stored his van. "Mrs. Bergen sure didn't waste any time to start getting rid of my stuff; I'm all paid up till the end of the year. You cannot do this." Jerry adamantly tells the two young guys standing by.

They had already removed the big garage doors. A big yellow bin was taking up most of the lane. The rest of the building was just going to get torn down after these two had removed the saleable. And the garage doors were worth something and peering around Jerry can see most of his stuff was gone except all the seats and other van fixtures. They have been disturbed though, and Jerry is sure these two guys have seen value in them. Again, Jerry holds up his hand.

"Sorry guys but that stuff is all mine. Do not touch another thing. I'll have a word with Mrs. Bergen then you two can help me load these in the van." The two young guys say nothing as Jerry turns to leave them.

Mrs. Bergen's face is framed in the glass of her back door. A vision Jerry has seen a hundred times before, when coming up on her back stairs. Without knocking Jerry pushes the door open and goes inside.

"What's going on? I paid you until the end of the year."

"Oh, Jerry I'm so sorry, we hadn't seen you, so we thought you had just moved on. I've had lots of tenants that just go without notice and leaving all their things too. You know that."

"Not if they've already paid their rent?" Seeing the stricken look on her face he toned it down a bit.

"It isn't your fault Mrs. Bergen. I bet your niece Adele, is helping you out with this. So, what's the plan are you pulling the house down too?"

"I don't know really but I'm told we're going to build a little house back there and a nanny will live in it and look after me." Smirking Mrs. Bergen tells Jerry she refused to move into the care home. Instead Adele hired a live-in babysitter to stay in the basement until the lane way house could be built.

"By then though I might be dead..."

"Well at least you won't have to go to the care home." Jerry mutters sympathetically. Jerry looks out the window and sees the two guys getting restless, so he says his good-byes to his landlady: but not before getting his rent and deposit money back. In cash too, which was a bit of a shock that she keeps so much on hand.

When out in the lane again Jerry tells the two workers if they give him a hand, they can keep most of the other stuff of value, he sees they already took. The guys happily help him get the van seats installed, the table back in place and a few other things that need going back into their original position and then he is on his way.

His appointment was at 4:30 but taking a chance he arrives forty-five minutes early and sure enough his van drew a crowd. The man doing the appraisal sails out of his office to introduce himself.

"Hello, I'm Mr. Sadowski ... sorry I never caught your name when I spoke with your friend Dave - and you are..."

Pops wondered what or why a person, now a days, needed to put a title before their name during what ought to be a casual interaction; he wondered what other footage this would give. Nearly always introducing himself to others using his first name - this time he says, "Its Mr. Landvik."

Mr. Sadowski circled the van opening doors checking for rust. He looked at the service records.

He got one of his mechanics to hoist it up and look at the under carriage and under the hood. Then he sat Jerry down to tell him two things. The first is, he may have a buyer and Jerry can consign it for sale through the dealership. In other words, Mr. Sadowski would take a commission of thirty percent.

Next, he told Jerry it was rare to find a mint condition van in original shape. One kept undercover for fifty years; unbelievable. And the price Jerry could charge was unbelievable too.

"Does this appraisal come in writing..." was all Jerry wanted to know. Then thanking Mr. Sadowski and paying an appraisal fee, Jerry makes his way back to the bike shop where he hopes Geoff will be waiting.

GEOFFREY STOPS in at his Gran's, even though this was going to be a cooking day with her granddaughter. Charlene looks so happy when Geoffrey sees her through the window. And she looks so young too. She is wearing an apron over her usual clothes but right away Geoffrey notices, no makeup on and her hair is neatly done in two thick French braids down her back. Slipping into the little house without anyone noticing, he scares them both and a sleeping dog too.

"What are you doing here Geoffrey?" Charlene and his Gran say at once. Geoffrey is prepared for Charlene to be annoyed at his intrusion, but she instead blurts out with glee that Gran has a boyfriend. Mavis blushes deep into the roots of her hair and all down her throat. Charlene proceeds to tell Geoffrey about the guy on a bike dressed in cycling clothes. A very cool looking guy. She chattered on and on and finally said she is sure this man, Jerry, is the reason their Gran changed her look.

"To match Jerry's look. Geoffrey, he is so cool - for an old guy." Before they can continue Geoffrey's cell phone rings. It's Dixie. Just calling to make sure he will be home. "You bet!"

As he ended the call, he saw he a message waiting so he picked it up. It is from Pops wanting to talk to him by five. Looking at the time display on his cell he said he had to get going and would see them about Noon the next day. Driving like mad but not too far. Dave's shop's mid-way between Gran's and Dixie. He will stop, see Pops, and get home by six.

Geoff pulls up just as Pops is backing the van into Dave's shop. Geoff watches pops go through the standard routine. Pops turning off the ignition, wiping down the dash and giving the rear-view mirror a wipe too before hopping out. Pops jumps when he sees Geoff watching.

Stepping out of the driver's seat he asks Geoff to join him in the back. Pops opens the side doors of the van and Geoff is shocked to see a vastly different scene. Pops steps in first and sits at the little table, beckoning Geoff to join him and close the doors. Once seated, Pops asks,

"How do you like it – pretty nice when it's all cleaned up eh? Can you see yourself going on a trip in this van? I mean with me, someday?" Geoff felt flattered. He knew Pops had never gone away with his son and he felt this offer came from very deep down.

"I'd be truly honoured Pops."

"OK. I need to talk to you about something Geoff, so if you can just listen for a minute...I've got to sell this van. I need a big chunk of money and I have a proposition for you." Geoff sat and listened in disbelief while Pops asked if he would like to co-own the van. He showed him the appraisal and told him about the commission. Saying he wanted to sell Geoff half the van for half the appraisal minus all the commission. "I know it's a lot of money, but I want you to have first crack.

"And Geoff when I die, the van would automatically go to you and you can do what you like with it - sell it or keep it. I just can't think of anyone I would rather leave it to. And I would do that, except I need some money now and I don't need the commitment of owning the van any longer. Right now, I want to make a different kind of commitment."

"But Pops why do you need the money? I could help you out a bit. Are you sure you want to sell the van? That seems so drastic." Geoff was touched but didn't want to take advantage and if there was another way, he wanted to make sure pops investigated it.

"No Geoffrey. Do you remember I told you if I had a second chance; a do over? I would sell the van. Well I have one." They left it like that with Pops saying he could give him a week or ten days to think about it and try to raise some money for this, "Once in a lifetime opportunity." When Geoffrey's about to leave, he leans in and gives Pops a hug of gratitude.

CHAPTER EIGHTEEN

The drive back home was done in a dream state. A dream of owning a V Dub '65 Classic. He felt as if he had stepped into someone else's dream or that Bonnie had talked Dixie and him into watching a made for TV movie featuring an irresistible happily ever after with a miracle at the end of the film.

When he started helping Pops, he did it out of an instinct to do so. His instant kinship with the man made it easy. And the fact that they kept bumping into each other also made it easy.

But Geoff was not the guy who thought of himself as deserving. He worked hard toward his goals never taking handouts from friends or family. His preference was to apply to bureaucratic strangers for grants and bursaries. He long considered this practice a guilt free option.

ARRIVING LONG after six that night, Dixie was not pleased. At the last-minute Dixie invited her aging aunts and all her sisters for dinner. The trip up the stairs stressed her aunts out and all suspected this would be a last trip to dine at this house. That very afternoon Bonnie announced she would not return to a degree program and instead intended to become an electrical contractor. This was news to everyone, but it would not be to Geoffrey.

Dinner was all but over by the time Geoffrey sidled through the door. His mood was subdued all through dessert. The group of women assume the visual reprimand they see from Dixie gave him something to think about.

But it's the van his mind is on. So, when Dixie presses him on what he thinks about Bonnie's shift in career he says, "I'm sure Bonnie knows what's she's doing." His comment gets a thumbs up from Bonnie, and frowns all around the table from the rest.

As for Dixie, it's the first sign that something besides her and her family is on Geoffrey's mind. Dixie knows – this something else, is why Geoffrey was late tonight. Most of the time Geoffrey tries to live in the moment. Right now, he is hung up in a moment that happened earlier in the day...but for some reason he remained there throughout dessert during the after-dinner chat and long into the night.

Geoffrey is in a distracted place Dixie's never known him to go. It was either a place in the past or way off in the future, but it certainly was not in the here and now. Instinct, quietly says, leave him to it. And so that is exactly what Dixie does...

$\sim$

FOR THE NEXT few days Geoffrey walks around as if in a wild hallucination. His head filled with weekend trips or day trips to Jericho Beach or Spanish Banks in the rain. He wants the van. It's been his dream...and he just didn't know yet how to make it a reality. He just bought a small car to get around in and all his money's gone.

Knowing Dixie will lend him money doesn't compel him to ask for a loan, however. And though he knows he should, he has not shared the news of the van offer with Dixie. This is something he wants to do on his own.

The biggest surprise in all his reverie, is he never adequately shared his desire to own a VW and go sight-seeing with Dixie or anyone except casually with Dave and to a larger extent, Pops. He has no idea if Dixie will share his desire to sneak off on weekend trips. Or could get turned on by the idea laying inside the van reading to the sound of coastal rain. Or if she would like a cup of coffee made right on the vans tiny stove? He pictures them sitting on a chair outside the van doors with sun shining down.

Geoffrey can see them both huddled under the comfort of a blanket keeping each other warm on a wintery day. Each with an enjoyable book and a bag of cookies, his Gran has made. He can see them as clear as a bell; but will she be able to.

He thought of Pops and the story he told of the van becoming a barrier for family connection. Pops said his love of the van, in reflection may have stood in his way of finding pleasure in about any other family affair. It was not a question that Geoffrey wanted the van. The first question was if he could live a balanced life with the responsibility of the van. The second question was where he would find the money.

SUNDAY AS PROMISED he picks up Charlene and all the food they have prepared. During the drive over Geoffrey is bursting to share the news and he's anxious to keep it to himself until he's been to the bank. So, his mind wanders as he drives and isn't paying attention to the other conversation that goes on beside him.

When he drives back to Vancouver after the memorial it's in a daze. He never paid attention to meeting and greeting the various friends of Robin's and won't be able to relay to his Gran what happened. If she didn't know him better, she might imagine he is having a delayed reaction to his grandfather's death. Mavis, just like Dixie, knows something else is up.

FINALLY PULLING UP, what his Grampa Stan used to call his, big boy pants, he goes to the bank only to be turned down. They said he had no credit rating and not enough discernible collateral. His new TA job didn't start for another couple of months and his contract with the library was about to end.

His last option is to ask his Gran. He feels sure she will lend him the money. The next day he calls her to ask her to lunch. "Oh no please don't take me out; you come here Geoffrey. There's someone I want you to meet."

"Gran, I need to ask you something and its personal so I'd rather just you and I were there. I have to ask you for a favour and would rather do it privately. Without an audience."

CHAPTER NINETEEN

Mavis feels shy about bringing her dog with her to Doreen's. Last week everyone in the family, except Charlene, had made fun of her attachment to her little guy. Saying she was "getting to be one of those old ladies."

What ladies she wondered; her daughter piped up before she could ask the question, "You know mum, old lonely ladies with no life." Her daughter treating her like she was a very dim child. Too dim to understand what they were getting at. But she got it all right. Doreen struggled but she had not had a drop of booze since a blow out with Charlene the week after Charlene went walk about and ended up at Mavis's.

Today felt like any other Monday, except for a change it was Sunday that Mavis has a nice meal packed tight inside her new cart. Mavis gets ready to go with a nervous sense of apprehension. She wears her best bright red pleated skirt, put a shine to her leather shoes and as she stands back to have a look in the floor length mirror, she thinks, I look rather good.

But today like every other Monday she has gone to

Doreen's; they will laugh at her about something and she just hopes it was not Jerry they laugh about this time. They never once said, "Thanks Mum that was great." Or "Can we give you a lift home..." or even "How about I pick you up?" The reminder of how thoughtless they are makes Mavis smile privately wondering if she really is a martyr.

Nope she never hears any word of praise but still every week since the big fight, and after the apology, and finally after the second grand apology, she had resumed her weekly trips. The biggest apology is the one that brought Doreen all the way to see her at her new laneway house for the first time. Doreen had seen the light she said, and she was going to try a life sober.

Mavis makes a vow to herself she will make the trek to Surrey at least once a month after today. Today's meal is perogies and cabbage rolls and in the future, she will be carting some other meal in hand. Mavis puts up with her family; it makes her feel good to put these meals together for them.

And every time, she spends time putting on nice fresh clothes before going to see them she does so out of personal pride, love for them and a hope she will lead by example. Now that Jack is in her life, she makes sure her new little friend has a good cleaning too before they make the journey.

JERRY ASKED HER LAST WEEK, "why do you do it?"

"It's what a mum does; don't you think so Jerry? It's what my mum did, and it is what I do too. My mum never would have put up with the back talk though. I blame myself for that. If I had stuck up for myself when I was married to

Doreen's dad, she would have seen I expected and deserved more."

Her girls would wonder what she was all dressed up for again and this time, for once, it was not only for her family or her own self-respect. This time it is in part for the deep respect she feels for Jerry. Today is a big day for Mavis.

Today Jerry finally meets the special grandson, or at least Geoffrey promised to be there. Originally he planned to come to the house to meet Jerry but when he heard Jerry was going along to meet Doreen, he decided he and Dixie would go there instead to protect his Gran and to protect her new friend Jerry too. The new person in his grandmother's life and the little dog brought her what she deserved; happiness and someone to love.

She thought of taking the SUV all the way to Surrey but by now she was so used to the bus she chose to stick to plan. And the SUV was getting something Geoffrey called a detailing. He wanted it to be returned in the same pristine condition she had always kept it in. Mavis so used to catching the bus to Surrey on her own, for some reason she wants to share the ride with Jerry. Plus, the thought of fighting traffic all the way there, is a turn off.

Besides, Jack has his own little carrier shelter bought especially for the bus. It fit snuggly right on top of her tartan shopping cart. There was a time she would have been appalled to have a dog anywhere near food but not her little Jackie. She loves him and he can do no wrong.

Since Jackie's come to live with Mavis or Maeve as Jerry calls her, Jack has never been so spoiled. It is as if they were meant to find each other and perhaps they were. By now she's heard the story of how Jack came to be Jerry's dog. She feels it was always meant to be that the three of them meet.

After hearing how Jack had been dumped at the pet

store by a young woman saying the dog was her parents; Maeve knows he is the same little guy she had found outside her gate, two years before.

Her shopping cart full, with dog kennel on top, it goes smoothly up the steps of the bus, on its specially designed wheels. Jerry fixed it for her when he realized she'd need something a bit sturdier to carry Jack. Smoothing out the hem of her red skirt, she watches as the bus draws closer to the stop, that she first met Jerry at. Pulling her red cardigan tight, making room for a familiar gent to squeeze in next to her. She feels his gaze and watches him peek inside her bag where the little tail of her white dog vibrates with pleasure.

"Nice dog; does he bite?"

"Oh no - he is as friendly as can be."

"Thought so. I've seen you two around." And with that, out of his breast pocket came a little blue polka dot bow tie. "For our pet" was all he said, but it was the kindness that prompted Mavis to take his hand and invite him, again, to her daughters for lunch. Squeezing her hand in his, Jerry threw a shaggy white head back and laughed.

The trip to Surrey went too fast. Mavis pointed out things of interest. Suggesting places, they could drive to in the SUV. Like the West Minister Quay. She had never been there, had Jerry?

They talked and talked until before they knew it the last stop loomed into view. "I really don't know why you would want to meet my family Jerry. I'm so worried they will be rude. Well, ruder than usual." She gave a nervous snort.

"Not to worry my dear, I have the skin of a rhino. I've had so much pain in my life there is nothing that can hurt me now." Stroking the back of her hand he says, "Don't worry love, it'll all be OK." Jerry opens the dog carrier the moment they step off the last bus. He lets his little pal out for a stretch of the legs.

"Would you like to hold Jack or the shopping cart?" Mavis knew how much Jerry missed Jack, so she said "Cart." Smiling Jerry ties Jack's leash to the handle and tells Mavis he'll do both. "Here we are Jerry, just over there. Oh, and look who's coming to greet us..." said Mavis pointing.

Distracted by a sound behind them, Jerry hears a familiar motor; he turns to see his van, cruising slowly down the street. It parks and out steps the young man who bought the van. "Raising his hand to give a wave Jerry turns to say, "Hey that's my van." Maeve gave a confused laugh. "Really? Well - that's my grandson."

Before Jerry's son became ill, Jordan shared his mother's view that everything happens for a reason. Jerry took their belief with a grain of salt but now he believes them both. Dixie and Geoffrey walk toward the grinning couple. Geoffrey is baffled and looks it; with hesitation he extends a hand to Jerry "Hi... what's going on...what are you doing here Pops? I don't get it...Do you know my Gran?"

Looking at the couple holding hands, Geoffrey corrects himself "Well I can see you two do know each other, what's going on?" Still not believing his eyes it is Charlene running back out of the house and down the sidewalk shouting hellos and waving, "Hi Gran ...Hi Jerry...and Jack - Geoffrey - Dixie. I'll be right back – come on Jack let's go for a quick run. Can I take him?" Geoffrey and Mavis both looked shocked. Mavis is closer than she had ever been to nervous laughter.

"You're Jerry? Wow this is crazy, Gran. Pops and I – I mean Jerry and I already know each other." Turning again to look at the man he knew as Pops all dressed up and looking like a new man. Geoffrey says, "So it's Jerry eh?"

Turning back to his gran he takes her free hand and tells her how he met Jerry at the library.

"It's his van I bought... Pops my Gran gave me money to buy your van. How strange is that? Did you know it was his van Gran?" Geoffrey could see his Gran is as baffled as him. "Gran this is the guy I wanted to introduce you to – this is Pops."

Feeling unsettled by this revelation Geoffrey and Dixie and, Maeve, as Jerry apparently called her, congregated on the sidewalk where they piece together this strange coincidence.

It is Dixie in the end who says, there was no such thing as coincidence. "I don't believe in coincidence - everything happens for a reason..."

Dixie pulls Geoffrey by the hand and together they go ahead into the house while Jerry waits with his Maeve for Charlene to return with their dog. "Maeve, I have something more to tell you as if knowing Geoff isn't enough. I bought your ring with the money I got for the van, well a small fraction of it. You bought your own ring in a way. How odd this day is turning out to be?

"There they come." Pointing up the street, Charlene is running along with Jack jumping up at her side. "Take me inside to meet the rest of your family. Come on Charlene," Jerry calls out, "bring Jack inside now, and introduce me to your mother."

SHYLY CHARLENE TAKES her grandmother's arm as they enter the house. Holding out her hand for the cart, Mavis begins to unpack while Jerry is ushered into the living room. This is how they had rehearsed it last weekend when Charlene came for dinner. She said she wanted to introduce Jerry while her Gran busied herself in the kitchen.

It was so quiet in the other room; it was if no one was home. There was no noise of TV, just soft background music playing. Mavis peeked around the corner to see how it was going. Charlene must have instructed the whole family on how things would go today. The little boys wore clean clothes and were standing tall shaking Jerry's hand. Doreen had a look of twitchy new sobriety on her face and Bethany, well Bethany always knew how to act around strangers.

A few minutes passed and Mavis feels rather than hears, Geoffrey come up behind her. "Gran, why didn't you say you knew Jerry?" In answer she turned the face Geoffrey had always known; a face usually filled with concern for others, was now transformed. A radiant face lifted up to look into her grandson's eyes and she says, "Why didn't you? You call him Pops! How would I know and why didn't you know? And why on earth didn't Jerry know...

"Maybe we all have our reasons and maybe our reasons are the same. Distraction by attraction... I saw Jerry outside the store that day you drove me down to buy groceries...you were with me, but my heart went out to him. He was sitting on the sidewalk. He looked like any other homeless man who had been roughed up. I was shocked by his condition. I didn't quite recognize him.

"And Geoffrey, Jerry didn't seem to know me. I don't think I wanted to embarrass him, or I was embarrassed by him... I don't know. The next day I went back to try to find him again; you were driving around and around the block.

"I thought you must be looking for me, so I stepped out of sight watching as around and around the block you went. Now, I wonder were looking for Jerry? Is that right Geoffrey?

I just realized seconds ago." Taking Geoffrey's face in both her hands, she tells him that she loves this man.

"He is my soul mate; I've waited my whole life to meet him. I asked him to live me Geoffrey. And do you know what he did before he said yes? He sold his most precious belonging. He said he was making room for me to be the most precious thing in his life. He bought me a ring to seal the deal. He said he sold his old van to the young man he would have wanted if he had had a grandson.

"He told me about you. A young stranger who saved his life...he said we both did. Saved his life...He tells me over and over how lucky I am to have my family. And especially you! He envies me my family. As dysfunctional as we all are, he still wants to be part of us; he wants to be part of this family."

Geoffrey knew Pops had a girlfriend that he intended to marry. A woman named Maeve. He called her his little lady, his soul mate. They drove to a mall together right after Pops had sold him half the van. Pops asking, "Hey do you want to come take a look at a special ring I'm picking up for Maeve?"

Geoffrey had said "No. But I'd like to meet Maeve after she says yes though. Maybe you'll invite me to the wedding?" His world was changing before his eyes; his mother a bit shaky but sober and polite in the next room; his grandmother lighthearted, relaxed, and happy... and his friend Pops or Jerry?

Before they arrived at Doreen's, Geoffrey told Dixie he's planning to cut lunch short today so they can go to the bike shop. He wants to introduce Dixie to Pops and to ask Pops to join him on the maiden voyage in their beloved van. And now he hopes Pops can tear himself away from his soul mate long enough to go storm watching with Geoffrey in Tofino. Geoffrey knows it won't make up for the trip he never took with his son, Jordan. But he hopes it will help Pops create some new memories with someone who plans to stick around to share them.

Pops appears in the doorway of the kitchen. To Geoffrey he looks innocent and bashful and as happy as he had seen him look. Reaching out Pops places a hand on Mavis's shoulder and without turning Mavis says, "Geoffrey love would you carry these appys in... Just set them on the coffee table." Turning then she gives Pops a surprised look throwing her arms around his neck. To Geoffrey she gives a wink, a ladened tray, and a whispered thank you.

Geoffrey stands still for just a moment, tray in hand. He stands in awe, bearing witness to the tenderness that's been blooming between his Gran and Pop. Out the corner of his eye, Geoffrey catches the movement of his mother Doreen, shifting a few chairs around for guests. He can hear her sober, hesitant voice as she arranges the seating just so. The twins are quietly captivated with a card trick Geoffrey has seen Dixie do a hundred times.

Charlene pokes her head around the corner to ask if anyone needs help. And Geoffrey marvels at the world. His world. It is changing before his eyes and Jerry Landvik, the man he calls Pops is about to become a bigger part of it.

His thoughts are interrupted when he hears Pops say to his Gran, "Geoff is a fine boy Maeve. He has your eyes."

the end...

DEAR READER

I feel completely honoured that you took an interest in Jerry Resurrected. And I hope you enjoyed reading the story as much as I did telling it. If you happen have a bit of spare time and would like to share a review it would be gratefully appreciated.

Reviews are incredibly useful to authors. They provide insight for the author of what works and what can be improved. I value your thoughts .

You can review Jerry Resurrected and my other books on Amazon and Goodreads.

Writing a story that brings my characters to life is a labour of love. If you would like to hear about new releases please visit my website and follow me at www.SukiLang.com

Cheers,
Suki Lang

ALSO BY SUKI LANG

Finding Nine
Amazon | Indigo | Kobo | Smashwords

Jerry Resurrected

ABOUT THE AUTHOR

Suki Lang lives with her husband and small dog on Vancouver Island. A storyteller by nature she has a strong belief in miracles and a certainty that everything happens for a reason. This writer has no trouble finding happy endings for her characters.

www.SukiLang.com
amazon.com/Suki-Lang/e/BoɪLYɪXCɪW
goodreads.com/SukiLang

Email me at suziconfuzi@gmail.com